SUBMIT

- A Novel -

MARK PARTRIDGE

Dedication

For Layla

Acknowledgements

I am indebted to many persons for their help with this book. I benefited from early readers who helped shape the manuscript, especially Polly Brophy, Barbara and Geoff Wiggin, and my sister Kathy Partridge.

My sister Ella Winton was an invaluable and careful copy editor and proofreader. The errors that remain notwithstanding her efforts are clearly mine.

To my wife, Mary, who listened to readings aloud, provided incisive comments draft by draft, and pushed me through the tedious final yards to the finish line, words are insufficient to capture my gratitude.

Table of Contents

Part One

1800

Chapter One

Ships sailing northeast from Halifax, Nova Scotia, navigate a coastline as jagged as the blade of a two-man saw. At the far end of this serrated shore, a narrow spit of land resembling the handle of a giant ax separates the open ocean from a sheltered bay and village the Mi'kmaq call Chedabucto and the British call Guysborough. This remote place is a comfortable colony nestled beneath the Anglican steeple of Christ Church, a small white chapel where families marry their daughters at the altar and bury their dead in neat rows behind a picket fence.

In the fading light of afternoon, a young woman named Submit Leete walks home from Christ Church along a path beside the rocky banks of Chedabucto Bay. She stops on the beach, picks up an object in the sand, and holds it up for inspection.

Her youngest sister, Huldah, runs up to her. "That one sparkles. What is it?"

"I'm not sure. Could be a gemstone." Submit places it in the left pocket of her coat where it mingles with the other stones and shells she's gathered on their walk home.

"Perhaps it is good luck," Huldah says. "Perhaps it means you'll get married, too."

"You're silly."

Huldah skips in a circle around her sister. Submit ignores her and continues her even pace as if walking the length of a church aisle toward an altar. The sun warms them, but a cold breeze tumbles fallen leaves along the path ahead. Submit pulls her wool scarf tighter around her neck.

"It would be such fun to have a triple marriage," Huldah says.

"Two is quite enough."

"Why won't you get married too? You're as old as our brothers."

"Maybe they are too young."

"Maybe you are too old. I'll get married by the time I'm twenty-three."

"You're sure of that?"

"All the girls in town say you should marry before you're twenty."

"Do they?"

"And they say you are almost an old lady." Huldah jumps forward as if playing hopscotch. She pirouettes on one foot, lands in a wide-legged stance with her fists against her ribcage, and blocks Submit's path with her elbows.

"Why aren't you married?"

Submit looks past her sister up the path to Leete Manor, the white farmhouse where they live on a ridge overlooking the ocean. Must she explain this to a mere child? She steps close, pushes the locks of Huldah's blond hair off her forehead, and cups her chilled red cheeks with both palms.

"Father hasn't found the right man yet."

When the sisters enter their house, Huldah scampers toward the children's playroom, but Submit ascends the front hall stairs to her bedroom facing the bay. She pulls on the carved oak leaf handles of a dresser drawer, arranges the items she found on the beach in the compartments of a wooden type tray, and wonders: what sort of luck will these bring her?

She hangs her coat and scarf in a wardrobe cabinet and returns to the main floor of the house.

She finds her parents, Andrew and Sarah, seated in the front parlor near a low fire. They halt their conversation and turn toward her. Her mother dabs at her eyes with a white handkerchief.

"I'm sorry," Submit says. "I didn't mean to disturb you."

Andrew stands. "You're not. Come in." He steps aside to make a place for her next to Sarah. "We have news."

Submit sits beside her mother, holds her hand.

"It's sad news, I'm afraid," her mother says.

"Captain Grant's wife died this morning," her father says. "She was ill, and it got the best of her."

"The poor man is fifty-two and left with a house full of children," her mother says.

Submit sags back on the couch. Poor Captain and Mrs. Grant. She likes them. Mrs. Grant is kind, pleasant, patient with children. The Captain is a nice man. He asks questions and listens to her answers, as if he wants to know what she thinks. She has known them almost half her life, beginning when her family moved to Guysborough after the War. The Grants were one of the first families to greet them, bringing by fresh baked pie and a bottle of brandy. She grew up with their children. And they are now alone without a mother. The news of this death is sad indeed. What can she do to help?

"He'll need a new wife, of course," her father says. "There will be many women in Guysborough glad for that role. He may be fifty-two, but he's a brave and successful man. A good soldier in the War and he's done fine business in Guysborough since then."

"I'm not so sure there's as many as you think, Andrew. Most who fit the bill are already married."

Her parents speculate about the Captain's next marriage but Submit doesn't listen. Instead, she sorts through her mixed emotions, as if sorting shells and gemstones from the beach.

Chapter Two

The Reverend Peter De La Roche faces the congregation at the Leete's double wedding in Christ Church. Before him stand Submit's brothers, Jabez and Andrew Jr., in matching black suits. Jabez tugs at his collar and scratches his neck. Andrew shifts his weight from side to side. They stare forward at Reverend De La Roche.

In the first pew to the Reverend's right, Submit sits with her father and mother and her three younger sisters. Huldah, the youngest, wiggles in her seat next to Submit.

The mother of the two brides, Mrs. McPhearson, sits in the first pew on the Reverend's left with her three young sons. There is an empty spot for Mr. McPhearson beside her.

Friends and neighbors dressed in their Sunday best fill the remaining pews and lean against the back wall. Captain Grant sits with his seven children several rows behind the Leetes. Submit did not expect him to attend, but that's the way it is in their village—life goes on.

The chapel hums with the rustle of stirring bodies, soft whispers, coughs, and a sneeze. Then the church bell in the steeple begins to toll.

Filling the room with his booming voice, Reverend De La Roche delivers these words from Acts:

"And it shall come to pass, that whoever shall call on the name of the Lord shall be saved."

With that, the double doors in the rear of the Chapel swing open. Mr. McPherson escorts his daughters, Mary and Margaret, into the church. The brides wear matching long white dresses and carry evergreen boughs dotted with red berries. McPherson leads them to the altar. His daughters face Reverend De La Roche, Mary beside Andrew and Margret beside Jabez.

Huldah pokes Submit in the ribs. "You should be next," she says loud enough for most of the nearby congregants to hear.

After the ceremony, the guests gather at the Court House for a reception. White ribbons and spruce branches decorate the inside of the wood-framed building. Brandy and hot mulled wine warm cold revelers who dine on lobster rolls, cod fritters and oysters. Captain Grant's son, John, two years her junior, opens fresh-caught Virginicas, her favorite. She hasn't seen him since his mother's funeral and yearns to say something kind. But he's surrounded by others serving the wedding feast. Then she hears someone behind her.

"Hello Miss Leete." It is a soothing voice, deep, soft.

She turns and looks up.

"Oh, Captain Grant!"

She is a tall woman, but he towers above her by at least a foot. Despite the decades since the War, he retains his military bearing. He stands upright, with his chest forward and hands clasped behind his back. His trim hips and belly suggest a younger man.

"A lovely evening," he says.

"Indeed. Very."

She's unsure what to say next. Will it be light banter about his son's shucking skills? A note of levity about the out-of-tune musicians across the room? A clever comment about the morbid homily of Reverend De La Roche beseeching the young couples to let their love follow them into their grave? None of that seems right. His wife has died. He still wears a black mourning frock.

"Captain, permit me to say how sorry I am for your loss. Mrs. Grant was a wonderful woman."

"The finest there could be," he says.

"I have not seen you since the funeral. How are you and the children faring?"

"Doing our best." He looks away toward the musicians, where his young daughters dance with one another. "But the girls are so young. It's difficult without a mother."

Two women, a decade or more older than Submit, step forward to flirt. Submit knows that one is married, and neither looks very attractive nor well-dressed. Captain Grant is polite but uninterested. He excuses himself with a slight bow to Submit and heads toward his young children. Submit remains in an awkward circle of silence with the other women.

She turns away too, and sees her mother nearby, looking her way.

That night, alone in their bedroom, Andrew and Sarah review the events of the day. They agree it was a splendid wedding. Sarah and Mrs. McPherson both hope for grandchildren soon. They also laughed at Mr.

McPherson's performance on the bagpipe in his military kilt. It fit him well when he served in the Scots Guard, but now it looks overstuffed.

Andrew pretends to listen while he puts away his wedding clothes. With their two boys married, it is time to find good matches for the older daughters.

"How old were you when Andy was born?" he asks.

"You know I was twenty-two."

Andrew responds with a knowing grunt.

They have discussed this before and agree that they need to find a match for Submit, as she is the eldest. But it is not easy to find a suitable match in Guysborough. His daughter should marry an older man who can provide for a large family, not a young man with no means. No doubt his sons Andy and Jabez will struggle marrying at a young age, as he did, but that is what a young man should do, if he can. Settle down and raise a family with a young wife. But a daughter is different.

Things were better when he was older and married Sarah. He was ready then to have a family. He could provide for them. And she was only nineteen, less than half his age, able to produce the large family a man of means should have. That was the way to do it.

Submit should do the same. She would be a good match for any older man, of course. But it is the financial benefit of pairing her with Captain Grant that intrigues him most.

Sarah's mind turns to their daughter's future. A man like Captain Grant could provide a good living and more children. A woman needs children to be fulfilled. At fifty-two, Captain Grant is still a vigorous man. He's fathered children recently and should still be able to do so. After all,

Andrew was fifty-six when Huldah was born. Surely Captain Grant could provide Submit with children of her own.

Andrew climbs under the thick covers of the bed next to Sarah and feels her warmth. He can tell they are both thinking about a marriage between Captain Grant and Submit. A lot must happen to make this work.

He turns toward Sarah. They have voiced none of these thoughts this evening, but they know each other's mind.

"Do you agree?" he says.

"Yes."

"So, you'll talk to her?"

"Yes."

"Good. I'll work things out with the Captain."

"We better do this soon," Sarah says. "Did you see the other women at the reception?"

"Like flies to a fresh wound."

"Exactly, and none of them as suitable as our dear Submit."

Chapter Three

On Saturday, the morning after their monthly meeting at the Masonic Lodge in Manchester, Andrew Leete and Captain William Grant meet at the Captain's new sawmill on the banks of the Milford Haven River upstream from Guysborough.

William strokes the sharp teeth of a large circular saw blade.

"This arrived from Birmingham last week," he says. "No doubt the finest saw in Nova Scotia."

Andrew nods with approval—as an investor in the mill, he favors progress. But this is not the topic on his mind.

"How are things with the family?" he asks. "With the children, I mean." He is a man of deliberate thought. He prides himself in knowing what to say before he says it, but he finds this conversation difficult to form. No doubt a woman would be more at ease.

"Well enough, I suppose," William says. "They miss their mother. As do I."

"Do you think you'll remarry?" Andrew hopes this is not too blunt.

"Perhaps," William answers, showing no alarm.

Andrew presses on. "You know, I was nearly your age when I remarried. Best thing ever." He tries to adopt a tone of knowing wisdom. After all, he is old enough to be William's father.

"How so?"

"I found it a great blessing to have a young wife. She respected me and proved very productive."

William laughs at this.

"One is tempted to feel they have plenty of children already," he says. "Perhaps I am too old for more. Certainly, I'm not in need of more."

"Of course, I felt the same, but then along came Huldah. Quite a surprise, a welcome one of course, when I was an older man than you are now. She's a constant delight."

"Well, sir, I'm not thinking of that. But I do think the children need a mother."

"Of course, they do. And I dare say, one young enough to keep up with them."

William blows out the light of the lantern inside the mill, and the two men head outside into the afternoon sun.

"Tell me, Andrew," William says at last. "Do you have someone in mind?"

"That is for you to decide, of course."

"But?"

"But if you were to consider someone for the role, her mother and I would be pleased if you considered Submit."

That said, Andrew feels a rush of relief. Seed planted. Mission accomplished. But William turns to face him directly. He looks confused, surprised, as if this is something he cannot imagine.

Andrew places a hand on his shoulder. "Think about this, William. It would be good for you. And good for our business."

Back in the kitchen at Leete Manor, Sarah and Submit roll out dough on the flour-covered table in the center of the room. A large cast iron cauldron of water hangs on a hook above a fire in the nearby hearth. It steams and bubbles, adding warm humidity to the room. The women prepare savory lamb pies for a neighbor who has lost a newborn child. Both wear simple homespun dresses with white aprons and caps. Sarah uses the death of the neighbor's child to steer their conversation to her intended destination.

"I wonder what you think of poor Mr. Grant," Sarah asks.

"I haven't much," Submit says.

"Surely you have some impressions."

Submit presses the heel of her palms into a ball of dough.

"He is old," she says.

"Not too old," Sarah says. "Your father was twice my age when we married."

"How did you feel about that?"

"It was good to marry an older man. For many reasons. He had the means to care for me and for our family. And he was still young enough to produce one. Without too many demands. And without straying into the arms of other women. We've had many good years together."

Submit's eyes widen at her mother's unexpected candor. They have not spoken together of such things before. She deflects instead of digging deeper.

"I'm sure Captain Grant will find someone to marry if that's his wish."

"No doubt," Sarah says. "A woman would be lucky to have him, don't you think?"

Submit can see where this is leading, and she's not sure she wants to go there. How committed is her mother to this advance? Does she pursue it alone or with her father at her side? Submit has little hope that she can parry her mother's attack if her father is an ally. Still, she tries.

"I have noticed several women in the town who seem eager for that opportunity."

But her mother will not yield any ground. Instead, she hardens her stance, and slaps the dough in front of her to punctuate her ultimate point. "Your father thinks that woman should be you."

Submit stops kneading and bows her head. She has nothing to say that will not betray her impossible instinct to defy her father.

Her mother walks around the table, enfolds Submit in her arms, hugs her tight, whispers in her ear. "Think about this, Submit. It would be good for you. And for the family."

Submit shudders at these words, then collapses into her mother's arms. Tears fill her eyes.

Chapter Four

~

Andrew arranges a visit to the Grant's after a Sunday morning service at Christ Church. Sarah asks Submit's sister Lucretia to care for the younger girls and tells Submit to fetch a pie from the kitchen. "Wrap it well," she says. "Try to hold in some of the warmth."

Andrew helps his wife and daughter climb into their cabriolet. Then squeezes in beside them. Snowflakes float around them in the cold December afternoon. The coach horse steams and stamps, eager to go. William flicks the reins.

Mother and daughter gossip about the news learned at church that morning—a recent death, who will marry next, a cousin's visit from London, a shipment of fine cloth at the general store.

Andrew ignores most of it and focuses on the ride through the countryside toward Grant Hall. The village has provided a good home for his family. They have prospered from farming and trade. His alliance with Captain Grant has served both well, especially their sales of lumber and cod.

They have become good partners and friends, despite their differences in age and backgrounds. Andrew is a simple man, a puritan at heart, frugal in his ways, displaying the reserved sensibilities of the New Haven colony where he was raised. His house outside the Village of Guysborough is large, but plain, a white clapboard box with brick chimneys at each end. Captain Grant displays a fondness for the grander privileges of his station as a British Officer.

The carriage rounds a hillock. Grant Hall stands in the distance, the grandest house in the area. It resembles the New York mansion the British occupied after General Washington retreated to White Plains. Grant had admired it then and recreated it years later in the Nova Scotia countryside. Any hesitation Andrew may feel about his plans for Submit's marriage evaporate into the air like the carriage horse's breath on this cold day.

Captain Grant's daughter Martha, a young woman close to Submit's age, welcomes them at the door. She beckons them into the large front entry hall and helps them shed their coats. Submit admires Martha's lovely dress—a new style she's not seen in the Guysborough shops. They follow Martha down the hall past the portraits hanging on either side of the room. One depicts a woman beside a collie with hills in the background. The other a man in a military kilt holding the reins of a horse. Captain Grant's parents. The woman looks like Martha.

"Father is in the study, Mr. Leete," she says. "I believe you know the way. He asked me to send you in."

"Yes, of course," Andrew says. Submit notices that he shows no offense at the informality of their greeting. But that is no surprise given their business association.

"Submit has a fresh pie for you," Sarah says, then turns to follow Andrew to the study. "Dried cherry. I believe it's your father's favorite."

Submit follows Martha into the kitchen. Lily, the housekeeper, hunches over the kitchen table organizing—sliced cold mutton and hot soup. Steam rising from copper pots on a cast iron range triggers Submit's envy. They still cook at an open fireplace at Leete Manor. Lily pauses and wipes her strong black hands with a white towel.

"Hello, Lily," Submit says. "The soup smells delicious."

"Thank you, Miss Leete," Lily says. "Some say the smell of roasted onions makes a house a home."

"Submit brought pie, Lily," Martha says. "I hope everyone else eats too much mutton so I can have seconds."

Submit sets the pie on the table and lifts the cloth. Lily inspects the lattice work of the crust.

"A work of art," she says. "You'll make someone a fine wife one day."

Submit is taken aback. Is Lily in on her parent's scheme or merely mouthing polite platitudes? Regardless, she greets the compliment with a gentle smile.

"Let's see what the children are doing," Martha says.

They head upstairs to a large sitting room at the rear of the house. The younger Grants busy themselves with reading, drawing, and sorting a collection of shells laid out on the floor. Submit and Martha watch from the open doorway. The room extends from the main section of the house like a pier into the harbor. It's a long room ending in an octagonal shape. Each wall hosts large palladium windows offering views of the estate. More paintings hang on the walls—landscapes, still lifes, portraits. A pianoforte stands at the far end of the room.

"They're not always like this. Father told them to be on good behavior for your visit."

"How are you managing?"

Submit immediately regrets these words. Was it bad manners to allude to the loss of Mrs. Grant? But Martha doesn't seem to mind.

"We get by. Lily and I share duties herding this hoard. Isobel is very helpful. Mary has her moments. But both can tend to themselves. Will thinks he can, but he's only ten. Mother was on a two-year plan with Will, Barbara, and Donald, and they're tight as thieves."

Submit blushes at the notion that a woman could plan such things.

Martha and Submit step closer, and Will jumps to his feet.

"Hello, Submit."

He grabs her hand. She glances back at Martha, smiles, then yields to Will's lead.

She asks, "What are you working on, Will?"

Barbara and Donald abandon their drawings and join Will in guiding Submit into the room.

"He's sorting," Barbara says.

The children settle on the floor surrounding neat rows of shells arrayed by color and size. Submit kneels beside them.

"They are quite lovely. Do you have a favorite?"

Will reaches forward. "This one. It's new. I don't like eating oysters much, but the shells are wonderful."

"A Virginica," Submit says. "I like the shimmering swirls of green."

Will beams. Barbara asks, "Do you like shells, Submit?"

"Very much. I collect them too. I'm also fond of rocks and fossils."

"What are fossils?" Barbara asks.

Will answers. "Old sea animals trapped in rocks."

"How do they get out?"

Will glares at his sister. "They can't get out, silly. They're dead."

Submit smiles. "That's right. They're fossilized. You can learn a great deal from rocks and fossils and shells."

"Submit, will you show us your collection?" Will asks.

"Yes, of course. Someday."

Mary, Will's older sister by three years, steps forward from the corner where she has been reading.

"I don't like shells," she says. "They're stupid."

Part Two

Chapter Five

The harsh winds of winter give way to the suggestion of another Spring. Submit sits alone in her room on the second floor of the house at her desk by the window. A box of gemstones and a ledger rest on the table before her. One by one, she selects a stone, polishes it with a cloth, and makes notes about its size, shape and color in the ledger. Her mother enters the room.

"Captain Grant is here to see you. He invites you to join him for a walk."

Submit did not expect any interruption this morning. She is not dressed for visitors. She starts to object, but her mother interrupts.

"Be quick," she says. "We mustn't keep him waiting too long." She touches the sleeve of Submit's faded smock. "Please put on something pretty and join us in the parlor."

"Who else will go?" Surely, she must have a chaperone.

"No one. Just you," her mother says. "Hurry."

Submit strolls with Captain Grant down the path that leads toward Guysborough. Shimmering reflections of the sun dance in the turbulence at the mouth of the estuary. Her new bonnet shades her fair skin. The new blue dress, bought for her by her father on a recent business trip, is snug at the waist. She hopes it makes a favorable impression. Captain Grant wears a long gray woolen coat over a pale blue vest. He walks with his hands clasped behind his back. He's quite handsome, for a man of his age.

They agree it's a beautiful day, although Captain Grant expects rain overnight. Then an awkward silence rises between them. Submit waits for him to lead in their conversation.

He looks up as if that helps him think, and finally says "The children enjoyed your visit. Especially your attention to William's shells."

"They are wonderful children," Submit says. "So well behaved."

"Mrs. Grant, of course, gets credit for that. I'm afraid I am always busy with business affairs."

"Yes, of course."

"And since she died, it has fallen to Martha to manage the children and the house. With Lily's help."

"I can well imagine the time and attention that takes," Submit says.

"Yes, I'm sure you can. You too come from a large family. Your mother says you have been a big help to her, raising your younger sisters."

"I've tried to be helpful," Submit says.

"Excellent experience," Captain Grant says.

What is he thinking? Experience for what? Working as a nanny? Is this a job interview? Why isn't he paying attention to her new dress?

When she does not reply, he says, "Perhaps I have expressed myself poorly, Miss Leete. I only meant to convey my observation that your response to the challenges of your situation has been admirable, much to your credit."

Submit bows her head. "It's been a group effort, a gaggle of girls growing up together."

Captain Grant nods but says nothing. They walk on and Submit waits for him to speak. It is his turn.

Finally, he says, "I think you have made an important observation. A thought that has also been on my mind. Our family too has benefited from a group effort. But that is about to change. Once again."

Submit looks his way. "How so?"

He turns to face her.

"This is the news I wanted to share with you. Martha is getting married."

"My goodness! That's wonderful news! Who is the lucky man?"

"Michael Harty. From Manchester."

Submit nods. "Not far."

"No. But she will move there soon, leaving Isobel as the woman of the house."

Submit looks away toward the ocean. Isobel is a fine girl, but only fifteen. The difficulties caused by having her in charge of four younger children are obvious.

Captain Grant continues. "Lily is a big help, but mostly with keeping the house, not with the children."

Is this what Lily was suggesting when they talked in the Grants' kitchen? That Captain Grant needs a mother for his children? Did Lily know Martha's plans? Of course she did. This conversation is at a fork in the road. Further discussion of Martha's marriage will lead to an outcome Submit is not ready for. She takes the other path.

"Lily has been with you a long time," she says.

"Yes, her mother worked for us first. I have known Lily since she was a child. We all came to Guysborough at the same time, at the end of the War."

"What brought you here?"

"I was a soldier in New York. Then the British surrendered to Washington. The War was over. So, we left New York. Hundreds of us came here, to Guysborough, although that isn't what we called it back then. Do you know where we got the name for the town?"

"Yes. Father told me. He knew Sir Guy Carleton when he was Governor of Nova Scotia. Did you also know him?"

"Indeed. Quite well. He's Lord Dorchester now, living in England. Hasn't been back to Canada for years."

"How did you meet him?"

"I was with him in New York when the War ended. He was the Commander in Chief for the British then. I went with him when he met with General Washington to negotiate the evacuation. I remember it well. Washington wanted the slaves freed by the King returned to their masters in the South. Sir Guy refused. He insisted that all the slaves freed by the British had the right to leave as part of evacuation. Washington was furious but Sir Guy was steadfast. In the end, Sir Guy prevailed, and the freedmen left with the British evacuation."

"Lily and her family were part of that?"

"Yes, I remember the last day. The terms of evacuation were settled. The British were to return control of New York to the Rebels at noon. One clever soldier left a parting gift. He nailed the Union Jack to the top of the flagpole over the fort and greased the mast with pig fat. We all had a laugh at that. And then we boarded our ships and sailed north. About three thousand people, all headed for various places. About seven hundred and fifty of us sailed here on several ships. Soldiers, citizens, women, and children. Over two hundred freed slaves and their families. That's when I met Lily and her parents."

"That was a few years before we came?"

"About four years, if I remember correctly."

"How old was Lily?"

"Perhaps sixteen."

"Is that when she came to work for you?"

"Her mother did. Lily helped sometimes. Mrs. Grant had met them on the ship and liked them. Mrs. Grant needed help while she minded the children, so she took on Lily's mother to tend to the house. It worked well."

Captain Grant does not advance the point as if waiting for her to take the bait. Instead, she takes a seat on a bench on the rise above the River.

"What was the War like?" she asks.

Grant sits beside her. Both look toward the Sea. "It was a terrible thing," he says. "Many men died. The colonies were torn apart, sons against fathers, friends against friends. I believed the colonies should have stayed together under the English flag. Resolved their differences with the Crown without bloodshed. But others like Adams and Jefferson and Franklin were hotheaded. They chose liberty over submission. And so, we were forced into a war we didn't want. I was a soldier. I did my duty, I thought, to keep the colonies and England together. Unfortunately, we failed."

Submit turns to face him. "I like that you were loyal, that you did not betray your King."

Grant smiles and nods. "I like to think so." He stands and offers his hand to assist Submit. "In any event, we cannot change the past. We are here now—a jewel in the King's crown—enjoying the good fortune of our place and our family. I am satisfied with that."

Submit looks away. Can she be satisfied with that? There is symmetry in this convenient unspoken plan. Captain Grant finds a new Mrs. Grant to tend to the children while Lily follows her mother's role as keeper of the house. It worked well once. He must think it would work well again. No doubt her own parents would agree. But what about her? She feels resistance. She imagines a different future. Not as an unpaid nanny to children from another woman's womb, but as something else. Something hazy and uncertain, but something else.

Submit sits in a middle pew with her family and stares ahead at the open casket in the front of the church. A tuft of white bonnet pokes out above the sides of the wooden box. The corpse of Isobel Grant lays inside.

So sad, she thinks. Only sixteen. Running with Huldah two weeks ago on the path beside the estuary to deliver Valentine Day cards. Then caught in the rain. Then spiked with fever. Then dead. So sudden.

Reverend De La Roche's voice booms from the pulpit, strong and grave.

"The ways of God are a mystery. But they are good, and we can take solace in the knowledge that God has called young Isobel to a better life with him in heaven."

He continues but Submit's attention drifts off. In the front near the pulpit, Captain Grant sits erect beside Martha and the younger children. They fill an entire row. The youngest are squirming and bumping shoulders. Martha reaches over to stop them. Captain Grant does not move.

Lily sits toward the back of the church beside her husband George. They look noble, both with strong jaws and broad foreheads, heads held steady and erect. Why have they not had children? Is this why? This lesson in the arbitrary death of the young and innocent.

But children are a woman's duty to the glory of God. Heavenly Father wills that women bear the pain of having children, in their birth and in their death, the Reverend said. And yet Lily has no children of her own. The ways of God are mysterious indeed.

After the final hymn, Andrew leads the family out of the church. Submit holds Huldah close. She is limp, without energy. What must she be thinking, seeing death come so close to her, taking away her friend? What will this mean to her? And what does it mean for the Grants?

"And for me?" She voices this final thought and is abashed when others turn to stare.

That night after dinner Submit sits alone in her room looking out the window at the reflection of the moon on the estuary.

Her mother steps up to the doorway and taps her knuckle on the frame. She enters, shuts the door behind her, and takes a seat on the bed.

"I know what you're thinking, my dear, I heard you at the funeral. Perhaps you don't know you could be heard. But I heard. I know. I understand."

"Understand what?"

"You know it is time. The right time. Your father will speak to him tomorrow."

"I'm not sure about this, Mother."

"I think you know it is the best thing now."

"How can you be so sure?"

"Because I also lived this, with your father. God called me to comfort him when he was alone. You too are being called by fate to this. To do the same."

Her mother reaches over to touch Submit's arm. Submit wants to recoil but does not. She wants to protest but does not. What is fate? Why would God plan this for me? Why can't he let me be? What does he care?

"Why me?" she says.

"It is your good fortune to be the right person at the right time," her mother says. "We both wish this for you, your father and I. Can you deny that? Can you deny that everything adds up to that?" Submit's mother strokes Submit's hair, then cups her chin with the palm of her hand. "You will make us happy by doing this. And you will learn to be happy, as I have been."

"How do you know this?"

"Because I am your mother. And you. You are my daughter." She clasps Submit's hands in hers and holds them tight.

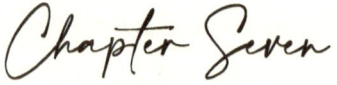

Andrew Leete and Captain Grant sit at a corner table in the Black Horse Tavern in Manchester. A young woman with ringlets of red hair trailing down her left cheek sets pewter mugs of ale on their table.

"So, it is settled, then," Andrew says. "We will hold the wedding in June."

"That suits me," Captain Grant says, lifting his tankard to meet Andrew's with a solid thud.

"There are other details we must settle, of course." Andrew swallows a slug of ale. "I am an old man, and you will no doubt outlive me. I want assurances that Submit will be well cared for after I am gone. We need to modify our arrangement for business succession. As things stand now, you will get full ownership of the fishery and sawmill when I die."

"As will you, if I die first."

"Unlikely."

"Possible."

Andrew dismisses that proposition with a flick of his palm.

"In exchange for Submit's hand in marriage, I want a few things. We must agree that she will have full ownership of the businesses when you die. And the house. And an income for life from the remainder of your estate. Can you accept that?"

"By right, that will all go to John."

"Unless that is changed. He has joined the military. You say that is going well. He will find his fortune there. We can secure a good post and rank for him. Whatever his destiny, let it lie in service to the Crown."

"Can I be assured that the younger children will be cared for?"

"Submit already loves them. She will care for them as for her own. We'll confirm that in writing if you wish."

Captain Grant looks up at the ceiling. There is a bird's nest in the rafters. Probably empty. Finally, he turns to Andrew and says, "I'll need some time to think about this."

Andrew smiles, and the men shake hands as if completing the purchase of a new saw blade.

Chapter Eight

Submit and her sisters walk along the path from their house down to the beach. They pass yellow patches of daffodils and clumps of forsythia. The branches of a magnolia tree in the pasture bend under the weight of abundant pink blossoms.

They approach a tangle of gnarled stems beginning to bear leaves.

"These rose bushes need pruning," Submit says.

"You're avoiding the subject," Lucretia says.

"No. Merely changing it." Submit gives her sister a playful push on the shoulder.

Eunice pushes forward. "But seriously, how do you feel about Captain Grant? Really?"

Submit turns toward her sisters. "Seriously, I think he's a good man."

"He's successful enough and still handsome," Lucretia says.

"And intelligent and thoughtful, in a gruff sort of way," Eunice says.

"Perhaps Mother and Father are right, I should be married."

"But? I hear a 'but' in there."

Submit scrunches up her face. "He's old," she says. The girls all laugh.

"Of course, he is," her Lucretia says. "But that's not a bad thing."

"It will be good for me and for the family, I suppose."

The sisters walk on. Submit weighs her decision in silence, then stops.

"I should be glad to marry him," she says, as if it's a question. "It is my duty."

"Can you love him?" Lucretia asks.

"Maybe."

"Honor him?"

"Of course, he is an honorable man."

"Obey him?"

"Yes, if his commands are kind and just." Submit's tone suggests she may even have a choice in this.

Eunice gives her a sly look. "Will you submit to him?"

"I hope so," Submit answers. The girls giggle again. Huldah pats her on the belly, then runs off with Submit in pursuit. The ruffles of their loose spring dresses flap in the breeze.

The day before the wedding, Submit searches the house for Huldah. She carries a package wrapped in white paper and a bow.

She looks in Huldah's room. It is tidy, clean, simple. The quilt on the bed is snug against the frame. No sign of Huldah.

She checks the front parlor, the dining room, the kitchen. She finds Huldah behind the house seated in the garden on a wood bench, her back to the house, slumped.

"Huldah, are you all right?" she asks. She steps around the bench to face her.

Huldah looks up, wipes tears from her eyes.

Submit takes a seat beside her and clutches her small hand. "What's wrong?"

Huldah sniffles, then says, "How can you leave me?"

Submit smiles. "You wanted me to get married, remember?"

"I don't anymore."

"Why?"

"I don't want you to leave. You're the only one who cares about me."

"I'm not the only one who does."

"You're the only one who understands me."

"I won't be far away. You can see me as often as you want."

"Mother says I mustn't. That I need to leave you alone because you'll have a new husband, a new family, a new life to take care of."

"She's wrong. I'll need you. I can't take this on without seeing you often."

Huldah says nothing, stares forward.

Submit lifts the package she's set on the bench beside her. "I have something for you."

"What?"

"Open it and see."

Huldah pulls off the bow and tears apart the wrapping, revealing a flat wooden box, the size of a large book. "What is it?"

"Lift the lid."

Inside is a quill pen and sheets of blank paper. Huldah looks up. Submit sees confusion on her face, replacing the tears.

"You can write letters. Write whatever you want."

"Who will I write?"

"Whomever you want. Write to me if you wish. Whenever you miss me. Father says it helps to write what you think, how you feel. It helps you understand."

"Do I need to give the letter to you?"

"Only if you want."

"I might write something bad."

"That's fine. You can give it to me if you want, or not. Whatever you want."

Huldah lifts the pen and thumbs the edges of the sheets of paper. "I like this very much," she says. "Whenever I use it, I'll think of you."

"Good. I'm glad." Submit pulls her sister close, feeling pleased when Huldah melts into her embrace.

Hours before dawn on the night before the wedding, Mary stands in the front yard of her house in the rain. The wet, thin cloth of her nightshirt clings to her skin. Why is her mother not there, standing beside her? She was there moments ago. Holding her hand. They walked in the afternoon sun carrying a lunch basket to her father's office at the mill. She spins around. There is no basket. No sun overhead. It was all a dream. But it was more than a dream, a fantasy of imagination, a vision of the future, a glimpse of the past, as real as life.

Chapter Nine

❧

The day of the wedding smells fresh after an evening rain. The June sun illuminates the facade of the white church. Flowers bloom beside the nearby graves in the church cemetery. The newest stone marks the final resting spot of Isobel Grant.

Captain Grant stands erect near the altar facing the entrance to the church. Some friends and neighbors sit in the pews. But mostly it's only family members—Grants and the Leetes. Lily and her husband sit toward the back where they sat at Isobel's funeral.

The gathering has a somber air, the atmosphere of a funeral, but for the absence of a casket. There is no music. The guests wait and whisper among themselves. They fall silent when the doors of the church open. Andrew Leete walks in with Submit holding his arm, her face covered with a veil.

Andrew delivers Submit to the hand of Captain Grant, then sits in the front pew beside Submit's mother.

The wedding couple turns to face the altar. Reverend De La Roche says a brief prayer for the congregation and begins the ceremony. Much of this is a blur in Submit's mind but the words of Ephesians seize her full attention.

"Wives, submit yourselves to your own husbands as you do to the Lord. For the husband is the head of the wife as Christ is the head of the Church, his body of which he is the Savior."

Beseeched to do so by De La Roche, Submit agrees to love, honor, and obey William "until death do us part." She lifts her veil, and the Captain places a gold ring on her finger.

De La Rouche raises his hand in an appeal for the attention of the congregation.

"I give you Captain and Mrs. Grant."

Submit and her husband turn to face their guests. She sees the broad smiles of her parents signaling their approval and happiness. The rest of the wedding guests look unsure, which is how she feels. Anxious and unsure.

Captain Grant leads her out of the church. She turns her head toward the Grant children when she passes them. The scowl on Mary Grant's face makes clear how she feels about this union. Submit looks forward. *I'll show her. I'll make the best of this.*

The wedding party and guests leave for the reception. Mary Grant lags behind and wanders over to the edge of the church graveyard. Fresh hyacinths decorate the graves of her mother and her sister Isobel. Nearby are plots reserved for other members of the Grant family. Mary bows her head in prayer. Two neighbor ladies walk nearby. She keeps her eyes on the family graves, but can hear each word.

"Isn't it a shame that such a beautiful girl is marrying such an old man," one of the ladies says. It is a young strong voice that Mary doesn't recognize. The woman continues, "She should marry a man her age, so she can have a family."

"She'll have a large family," the other woman says. "Captain Grant's house is already full of children."

"How will she manage?"

"It's bad enough marrying a man twice your age. But taking on a house full of another woman's children, that's unimaginable."

"Imagine."

"I can't. It's too dreadful."

"She's marrying him for the money, of course, nothing more. It's a marriage of convenience for him and a marriage of avarice for her parents. Captain Grant has plenty of money, and her father wants it."

"Esther! That's unkind."

"But not untrue."

"You're shameful."

"You'd marry him, too, if you could. He's not so bad for a man his age. Good looking in an old man way. And he's fit, he'll live forever."

"I don't think it will last."

"What will happen?"

"I don't know. But I do know this. Her father was married before, then divorced."

"Really?"

"Yes, and then he married Sarah. She was only nineteen when they married, half his age."

"What happened to the first wife?"

"She died eventually. But not before they were divorced. Perhaps it's in the blood."

"What? Divorce? Or death?"

The ladies chuckle at that and walk on. Mary stands still, staring at the family graves.

After a small wedding reception at the Leete's house, the Captain and Submit ride in a carriage to Grant Hall. Lily has put the children to bed and is cleaning up the remains of their dinner. She offers chicken stew but Submit is nervous and has no appetite.

The Captain says, "Thank you, Lily. We're ready to retire for the evening." He reaches out for Submit's hand. "Aren't we, Mrs. Grant?"

Submit lowers her gaze.

"Would you please show Mrs. Grant to our rooms?" he says to Lily.

"Of course."

Submit watches the Captain leave the room and then leans close to Lily. "What shall I call him? What does the Captain expect?"

"I guess that is up to him," Lily says.

"What did Mrs. Grant call him?"

"When I could hear, she called him Captain Grant. I don't know what she said when they were alone."

"Of course not." Submit wishes she had sorted this out before. It seems so odd not to know what to call him. But in a strange way, not focusing on that question made her less anxious about what lay ahead.

"What shall you and I call each other? I hope that won't change."

"You will still call me Lily if you wish. But when the Captain is near, I will call you Mrs. Grant."

"And otherwise? Will you still call me Submit?"

"Of course, if that is what you prefer."

Submit considers this and feels better. It's a lifeline to her own identity. Something to cling to as she becomes Mrs. Grant, an identity that seems to be that of another person. She stops in the hallway outside the bedroom door, turns to Lily, and takes her hand.

"Yes, Lily," she says. "I would definitely prefer for you to call me Submit, as you always have."

Lily smiles. "And thus shall we always be."

Alone in the bedroom, Submit undresses and puts on a white nightgown sewn by her mother for this occasion. The neckline is low but still demure. She settles into bed, propped up against down pillows with the quilt pulled up to her waist.

Before long there is a soft rap on the door. William enters and locks the door behind him. He stands still a moment facing her, then says, "You look lovely."

"Thank you."

"Are you scared?"

"No."

"Do you know what will happen?"

"Yes. No. I think so."

"You'll be fine."

He begins to remove his clothes, standing at the end of the bed. First, he drapes his black jacket on the back of a chair. Then he removes his shirt.

Submit watches him in the candlelight. His arms and chest are strong. His belly is tight, firm, flat. Like the shirtless young men she has watched working the fishing boats in the estuary. There is a scar across his chest, from his left collarbone to the right side of his left nipple.

"What is that?" she asks.

"From the War."

"May I touch it?"

He moves around the bed to stand beside her. She reaches up and runs a finger over the scar across his breast.

Chapter Ten

Submit soon molds herself to the Grant family routine and her role in the household. The Captain is up early and works in his study before breakfast. Lily arrives soon after dawn and begins to cook. Submit wakes the children, helps the younger ones get dressed, and brings them to the dining room. The Captain sits at the head of the table reading the latest news. She greets him with a kiss on his cheek. He smiles back.

Willy is the first to leave for the day, walking to the schoolhouse in Guysborough. Mary spends the morning with Barbara and Donald. She tutors them in reading and math, and joins them at play in the yard or the back parlor, depending on the weather. Lily does laundry, cleans the upstairs rooms, and readies lunch. Submit occupies herself with social correspondence—invitations, thank you letters, birth announcements.

In the afternoon, Submit takes Barbara and Donald to the estuary to hunt for shells. Or she helps Lily by taking the Captain's lunch to the mill or picking up a small order from the general store.

After school, Willy joins Mary and the other children in the playroom. They draw, nap or assemble a jigsaw puzzle. And Submit has time alone to read or write letters.

When the Captain returns from work, the family gathers in the main parlor before dinner. Donald, the youngest, insists on sitting on Submit's lap while she reads him stories. Barbara demands that Submit inspect her latest drawing.

Mary will have none of this. She remains distant, curt. One evening, Submit tries to engage Mary in conversation about her day. Mary says nothing, turns away, and leaves the room.

The Captain, seated nearby reading the Manchester Gazette, looks up. "Don't mind her, Submit. She'll come around."

Submit nods but keeps her doubts to herself.

Huldah sits alone in her room, sulking, angry. She has not seen or heard from Submit since the wedding. Even then, she ignored her. It was all talk. All a bunch of meaningless pander, that she would see her often. She's not come by once. And Mother won't let her go to Grant Hall to see her. How could she leave her like this?

She takes out the box Submit gave her before the wedding to write her first letter. She dips the quill in ink and begins:

"Dearest Submit."

She pauses. Her pet canary sings in its wire cage across the room. She turns back to the letter. Write whatever you want, her sister said. Write how you feel. All right, I will.

She fills the page with oversized letters:

"I HATE YOU!"

She stops to admire her work. "At least you were right about one thing," she says out loud. "It feels good to write what you think."

Even so, will she ever give this to Submit? She slips the letter under her blotter paper on the top of her desk and puts away her pen.

Part Three

1802

Chapter Eleven

❧

Submit lies in bed in the room where she first stroked William's scar. It is late and the room is lit by candles dripping wax on the tables beside the bed. Drops of sweat cover her forehead. She tenses. A wave of pain flows through her body. It starts at the pit of her belly and spreads out to the tips of her feet and hands. She clenches the muscles in her face. Creating pain on purpose distracts her from the pain she can't control.

Seated beside her, Sarah says, "That's it my dear. You'll be fine. It will be over soon." She lays a damp cool cloth on Submit's forehead.

Lily stands at the foot of the bed and reaches forward with both arms between Submit's widespread legs. "I can see its head," she says. "Push, Submit. Push."

The pain increases. She pushes through it, and then it's gone. She hears a gurgle and a cry and opens her eyes. Her mother holds a baby, wrinkled, red, coated with white like a loaf of bread powdered with flour.

"It's a girl. And she's perfect." Sarah lays the baby on Submit's chest.

Lily ties two pieces of thread around the umbilical cord. Then cuts through the tough connecting tissue with a sharp kitchen knife.

Submit cuddles her daughter against her skin. The baby puckers her lips and tries to suck on something she hasn't yet found. Submit says, "Hello, Elizabeth. Do you like your name?" The baby wails and the women laugh, a moment of humor to break the tension lingering after a night of labor.

But then Submit's smile slips away. Elizabeth is lovely, but what will William think? He wanted his first child born from her womb to be a boy. Their daughter is perfect, indeed, but will that be enough?

Weeks later Submit is in bed when William returns home. Submit lies on her side facing the crib with her back to the door. A single candle flickers on the table beside the bed. Elizabeth sleeps in the crib in the corner of the room, peaceful and quiet.

William says nothing when he enters the room. Submit can tell he is trying to be quiet, but she hears him bump into the chair by the door and stumble into the room. The bed breaks his fall. He sloughs off his clothes and lets them drop to the wood floor, first his boots, then his heavy coat and pants. Submit listens but continues to feign sleep. He slips under the sheets and moves close to spoon her body. His hand is cold on her bare arm, and he smells of tavern smoke. His hand drifts over her swollen breast. Crosses her still flabby belly. Comes to rest on the tender places between her legs.

She clutches his hand and guides it away from her body. "Not tonight, William."

He ignores her words and kisses the back of her neck.

"Not now," she says. "I'm tired."

"This will help you sleep," he whispers.

She turns to face him and pulls a pillow between them. "I said I'm tired. Yesterday I was up all night with Elizabeth while you slept. She needs to sleep now and so do I." Her voice is firmer than before, but she still tempers it with softness and concern. A plea not a demand.

Part of her feels she should be more compliant. But she can't bring herself to that now, and she can't risk disturbing the baby. She expects him to say something, to cajole or scold. He's frustrated, but he won't yell. He's not a hothead, and he's not unkind.

He purses his lips and rolls away from her onto his back. He rubs his face with both hands, then gets up, grabs his clothes from the floor, leaves the room, says nothing. Baby Elizabeth stirs when the door slams but returns to her peaceful sleep in a moment. Unable to copy her example, Submit stares at the candle flame until it extinguishes in a pool of melted wax.

Soon after her fourteenth birthday, Mary Grant takes lunch to her father at the sawmill. When she get near, she smells sawdust and hears the large circular saw cutting through wood. Inside the mill, Lily's husband George guides the side of a tree through the whirling blade. He is a strong man, broad-shouldered, skin as black as a moonless night in the country. He waves to her but remains attentive to his work. She shouts a greeting but knows he won't hear over the din of the saw.

She looks for her father in his office, but he's not there. She leaves the lunch basket on his desk and checks outside for his horse. She frowns when she finds the shed empty. She wants time alone with him, away from the distractions at home—the crying baby, her noisy siblings, Lily's watchful eyes, Submit's self-absorbed indifference.

She goes to the back of the mill where they stack cut boards on a dock jutting out into the estuary. She likes this spot near the water. She can enjoy solitude there. Wait for her father's return. Dangle her legs over the edge of the dock thinking about sloops sailing to places she's never seen.

She expects to be alone there now but is not. Instead, there's a boy her age building a pile of lumber at the water's edge.

"Abijah. What are you doing here?"

The boy turns and smiles. He slaps his gloved hands against his pants. Flecks of sawdust cloud around him. Although it still feels like winter, he has left his coat unbuttoned. His high-cheeked face is damp with sweat.

"Don't you know? I work here now. Whenever I'm not in school. I thought your father might have told you."

"No, he said nothing about it. But I suppose I wouldn't expect him to. These days he's so busy with other things."

"Do you come by often?"

"No. I am only out helping Lily by bringing him lunch."

"He's gone off with Mr. Leete. They went over to Manchester to eat at the tavern."

Mary pouts, frustrated by her inability to complete her lunch delivery. But then she brightens as her mind seizes on this as a pleasant change of plan. "Well then," she says. "Are you hungry?"

Chapter Twelve

It's been a year since Submit's marriage. Huldah walks through town, head down, eyes on her feet. She's angry that she has not seen her sister alone for more than a minute. And she has rarely seen Mary since the wedding either. As best she can tell, Mary now spends her free time with her new boyfriend. Submit has Captain Grant. Mary has Abijah. *And I have no one.*

Huldah pauses at the General Store and looks through the window at the latest wares on offer. She and Mary used to linger here. Stroke the dress fabrics. Crave candies behind the counter. Wish their fathers gave them allowances so they could buy things. No more.

She walks home past the buildings along the docks. Past town hall. Past the doctor's house on Main Street.

At home she takes out her pen and a fresh page of paper.

Dear Mary,

I walked by the General Store today after school and was thinking of you. Do you remember when Mr. Smith looked away and we stole pieces of licorice from the candy counter? We were so bad when we were young, weren't we? But now we're older, aren't we? Next year I'll be fifteen, same as you. Can you believe it? Things certainly have changed, haven't they? Everything is so different. I miss you so, I'm so lonely. And to be honest, I'm so jealous. You have a boyfriend. And you have my sister as your new mother. She was my best friend, until she married your father. Now I'm not sure. Don't you love her dearly? I want to say you're so lucky. But you're not of course, with so many losses afflicting you—your mother, your sister—like Job in our Bible studies. So many deaths. How do you manage? I hope Submit is a comfort. She is someone who can understand you. That's something, isn't it? I always thought you understood me. I know she did. I wish the three of us could be together, with no one else. Wouldn't that be wonderful?

Your friend always, Huldah.

Mary continues to bring her father lunch, almost daily. But now she hopes he will be gone, busy with other things, so she has more time alone with Abijah. They sit on the dock facing the lazy river. Mary shares the trials she faces at home with her father remarried to a young woman who now nurses a new baby.

"I suppose it's my sister, or half-sister at least, but all I can think is that she's an intruder. I feel nothing for her."

"Perhaps that will change." Abijah draws circles in the water with a stick.

"I just wish she were gone. Both of them. We were sad when Mother died, of course, but we had grown content being alone, just our family, with no others." She hesitates to tell the full truth but thinks it. She was happy having her father to herself. That is what she wants. And Submit and the baby block the way.

"Maybe this will cheer you up," Abijah says. "I've had a nice surprise."

"What?"

"Are you sure you want to know?"

She punches him in the shoulder. "What is it?"

He flinches and pretends to be in pain.

"I don't think I'll tell you."

He rises from the dock as if to leave, but she grabs his coat and pulls him back.

"Tell me," she says.

He lets her demand linger, then releases a heavy sigh. "Well, if you insist. My father returned from Halifax yesterday with a new rowboat."

Her faces scrunches like a peach pit. She was hoping for more, something for her, something she could enjoy.

"I can use it whenever I want." He leans in with his face close to hers. " *We* can use it whenever we want."

That makes her smile.

A few days later, Mary waits on the ferry landing in town. Abijah rows across the estuary in his new boat. She gets in and faces him as he rows upriver from the beach. Mary has rarely been in a small, nimble boat like this. It's exhilarating to be on the water, away from land, away from her family.

Abijah slices the oars through the dark water. Upstream, he glides the boat into a cove. He releases the oars, lets the boat drift, and removes his coat. It's late afternoon and the sun is high and warm.

Mary leans over the edge of the boat and reaches into the water. There's something below the surface, hidden in the shadows. She leans farther, loses her balance and almost falls in. Abijah pulls her back. She lands on his lap. Her arms surround his neck, her eyes fixed on his. Their laughing stops.

She kisses him.

Chapter Thirteen

❦

Mary becomes a frequent guest at Abijah's house. It's small, cluttered, with only a few dark rooms. But she's happier there than when she is at home with Submit and all the children. Abijah's father, Lemuel Scott, is funny, wild, independent, not like her stuffy Loyalist parents. He makes fun of the King, plays music learned from Acadians on an accordion, sings songs in French. And he tells stories about pirates.

Over dinner one night, Lemuel tells Mary about his visits to Halifax. The tall church in the center of town. The grand streets. The busy docks with tall-masted ships. And the smoky taverns where sailors and pirates gather.

"That's where I saw him," Lemuel Scott says. "Captain William Pryor, the meanest pirate of all. He was sitting in the back of the tavern with his sword laid bare on the table beside a pewter tankard of ale. And I wondered, if you crossed him, would he laugh, spit ale in your face, or slash your throat? He was known for slashing throats and bashing heads. They say he's buried pots of gold along the coast, gold stolen from travelers and thieves alike. He puts their head in the pots to scare away any who have the misfortune of finding one. A pot just like that." He points his long finger at a large copper cauldron of boiling water in the fireplace.

After their first kiss, Mary and Abijah row the boat on the river whenever they have a chance.

"Let's look for pirate treasure," Abijah says. "You heard Father. He says gems and gold wash up on the beaches of Guysborough Bay. The cargo of sunken ships. Let's find some."

They explore remote coves and inlets together. They wade into dark green water,. Push their wet legs through thick seaweed. Sink their feet into the soft silt of the riverbed. Afterwards they lie on the sandy bank until the sun dries their clothes.

They collect interesting rocks, but no gold. But there are other things below the surface.

They land on a long gravel beach at the mouth of the Salmon River near Cooks Cove. The flowing river water erodes the clay and exposes the lip of a copper pot beneath the water's surface. Mary finds it when she wades to shore and kicks the sunken object with a bare foot.

Abijah digs the pot out of the muck and drags it onto the beach. They scrape out the soggy contents with a broken tree branch—some long bones, a piece of skull, strands of hair, and beads made from shells.

"Looks like a girl's head," Abijah says. "And those beads are wampum."

Mary pokes at the fractured surface of the skull with a stick.

"It looks like she was hit with a club," Abijah says.

"Where do you think this all came from?"

"Indians, probably."

"Or pirates," Mary says. "Let's keep the shells."

Mary practices a Handel etude on the harpsichord in the family parlor. The cross-hands positioning is a tricky challenge. Lily comes to the doorway and pauses to listen.

"That's lovely, Mary."

"I'm struggling with this one."

"You'll get it fine before long. Your father would like to see you. He's in his study."

"What does he want?"

"He didn't say."

"When?"

"He didn't say,"

Mary knows what that means. Immediately if not sooner. She closes the lid on the keyboard.

She walks through the formal front parlor and the entry hall. Her father's study is at the far corner of the main floor. The door is open. Inside her father reviews a stack of papers on his desk. She raps her knuckles on the door jamb.

"You wanted to see me?"

He looks up and smiles.

"Ah, Mary, yes, I did. Please come in. Have a seat."

Two Chippendale chairs face the desk. She chooses the one to her right and waits for him to continue. He holds something back, as if caught between treating her as a child and respecting her as an adult. She has watched him confront her brother John like this. But has not experienced it herself before.

"I'd like to speak to you about Abijah Scott."

She does not respond. He clears his throat.

"Yes, well, I hear that you have been spending much time with him. Alone. Is that true?"

"We are friends."

"Well, that's fine, of course. Abijah is a good lad. I like him. He's very helpful at the mill. It's just—." He straightens the papers on his desk.

"What is it, Father?"

"I want you to be careful, is all. Watch out for his family too. They see things differently."

"I don't understand."

"They're not Loyalists like us. They came from Massachusetts after the French and Indian War. They never signed a loyalty pledge."

"I'm not sure I'm a Loyalist."

"Of course you are! We owe a lot to the King." He waves his hand around the room. "We owe all this to the King."

She purses her lips. She knows what he's getting at. She's smarter than her years, but she's unwilling to give in to his point. She's also unwilling to take him on. That leads nowhere. She plans her approach with care.

"I'm not yet fifteen, father. I'm only a girl. I don't care about Loyalists and politics."

William seems taken aback by that, looks almost foolish. "Well of course not. But someday, it will all—."

"I'll be careful, Father, don't worry."

"Good. That's all I ask."

"May I be excused?"

"Yes, you may. I'm glad we understand each other."

She rises to leave.

"One other thing," he says.

"Yes. What is it?"

"I think it's time that you talked to your mother about boys."

"My mother?"

"Submit."

Mary stiffens. Submit is not her mother, but again she chooses to avoid the debate. She is getting off easy. He is not prohibiting her from seeing Abijah, although other fathers might.

"Yes, father, I will."

He looks pleased. "Thank you," he says.

She nods, but this conversation will change nothing. She will not talk to Submit about boys. And she will not be careful. If anything, this conversation only makes her even more interested in Abijah. After all, she kissed a boy, learned about pirates, and poked a girl's skull with driftwood. She's past the point of being careful.

Part Four

1803

Chapter Fourteen

February 2, 1803.

Dear Mary,

Happy birthday! How does it feel to be fifteen? Father told me something funny this morning about you and me. We're not just friends, you and me. But I'm your aunt and you're my niece. And you're older than me. Isn't that odd? I think it's funny. I hope you have a great day. Give Submit a hug for me.

Your loving "aunt,"

Huldah

Huldah reads in the dining room. A stranger arrives to see her father. She catches a glimpse of him when they walk to her father's study. He's dressed in a chestnut brown coat and dark riding boots, a much younger man than her father, with thick, black hair.

He looks her way when she passes by the open door to the study. He has a lovely smile. And dark eyes. She looks away and goes into the front parlor across the hall. She tries to read the new book Submit gave her for her birthday, *A Vindication of the Rights of Woman*, but her thoughts keep wandering back to their visitor.

Before long she hears the men's laughter, shifting chairs, heavy steps on the floorboards. The visitor and her father stop at the parlor door. She saves her place in the book with her finger, and stands.

"Mr. Partridge, permit me to introduce my daughter. Huldah, this is Mr. Ebenezer Partridge, newly arrived in our isolated outpost at the end of the world."

Ebenezer nods. "My pleasure."

"Huldah is our youngest and no doubt the last of our children. Probably the smartest of the lot, always reading something."

"I see you're in the midst of something now," Ebenezer says. "May I ask what has your attention today?"

Her cheeks feel warm. Is she blushing? "A gift from my sister." She hands him the book to examine.

"Ah. Mary Wollstonecraft. I dare say you'll learn many fine ideas from her."

"I've just begun."

"Please let me know what you think when you finish." He winks and smiles.

The men leave and she returns to her book, but she can't focus on the text. Her mind focuses instead on that smile. Later, up in her room, she takes out a sheet of paper and writes.

Dear Mary,

We had a visitor today. Ebenezer Partridge. Have you met him? A most handsome man. Most charming. Perhaps one of us should marry him. That's all I can think of since meeting him. Such a lovely smile. Such thick black hair. If Submit can marry a man—your father—twice her age, we could too, couldn't we. But of course, you're going to marry Abijah. So maybe I get to marry Ebenezer. I can dream, can't I?

Your best friend, Huldah

A week later, William walks with Andrew along a muddy dirt road to the tavern for a late lunch after their weekly meeting at the Masonic Lodge in Manchester. They take seats at a table toward the back.

Andrew looks at his pocket watch. "He should be here soon," he says.

"Tell me more about him," William says. "You haven't said much yet."

"I've only just met him, but he comes well recommended. When he came to call the other day, he presented a letter of introduction from Gilroy in Halifax. He's quite young, about thirty I'd say, but according to Gilroy he's already well established in Halifax as a merchant. The English shippers still have a difficult time getting their goods into Boston Harbor. Even now, twenty years after the War."

"I know too well. Many are robbed at anchor. And more than a few sunk afterwards."

"Quite right, I hear the same, and it's confirmed by Gilroy."

He removes a letter from his coat pocket and passes it over to William.

"Here, see for yourself."

William glances over the letter as Andrew continues.

"Young Mr. Partridge has set himself up as a middleman. The English merchants send the goods to Halifax. He takes them from there to Boston on ships bearing the American flag."

"What does he want from us?"

"He says he has orders for textiles, lumber, and cured fish from his clients in Massachusetts. He's looking for new suppliers. Here in Nova Scotia if he can find them."

"We can't do much about the textiles."

"But we can help him with the lumber and fish."

"Can he pay upfront?"

"We'll find out. This could be a good opportunity for us."

"Where is he from?"

"Western Massachusetts. Middlefield, I think."

"Hmmm. Upriver from Hartford."

Andrew nods. "I've been there a few times, before the War. Not much to see then. A place for trading with the Indians. Beaver, mainly."

"I wonder if he trades in furs. There's demand for those in London."

Chapter Fifteen

Within a few days, William Grant greets Ebenezer Partridge outside Grant Hall.

"A perfect day for riding," he says. "Looks like you found your way without any problem."

"Your directions were exact, sir. No problem at all."

"I thought we would head to the fishery first then finish with the mill. How does that suit you?"

"Quite well, sir."

William puffs out his cheeks and nods. He ponders whether he should let it go or say something. "Let's get past the formalities, Ebenezer. I'd prefer you called me William. No need for sir."

"Yes, sir."

William scowls.

"Sorry. The habit is hard to break," Ebenezer says. Both men laugh, then ride down the hill from Grant Hall. Ebenezer asks about the history of his businesses in Guysborough.

William says, "I got started with the fishery first, soon after I settled here after the War. The sawmill came a few years later. I had no background in farming, but I learned logistics serving in the Regiment. How to marshal supplies for the troops. How to organize men."

"I can imagine that was good training."

"The best. We secured supplies from Canada during the War. So I knew a bit about the resources available here, especially salted cod and lumber.

"I joined with some of the others who arrived when I did to petition for the license to run a fishery. None of us knew much about the business of fishing, but we had good help and learned quickly. Eventually, I bought them out. I relied on my servant, George, whom you'll meet shortly. He's been with me since I was stationed in Philadelphia. He's a good man. I trust him to manage the daily operations of both businesses."

They crest a hillock revealing a view of the estuary. "You can see the fishery over there." Grant points to the southeast at a collection of frame buildings on a spit of land jutting into the bay.

"It's called Helpman's Island, though it isn't actually an island unless the tide is quite high."

In the distance, the riders can see three ships docked near the buildings. Several men unloading wooden barrels.

"I'll let George fill you in on the operations. We'll take this path down to the harbor."

When they reach the bottom of the hill, William calls over a black man to join them.

"Hello, George. How are things going today."

"We're doing well, Captain. Busy. Ready to salt and pack."

"This is the man I told you about. Can you give us a tour of the operations?"

George reaches up to Ebenezer to shake hands. "Glad to," he says. "You know much about fish, Mr. Partridge?"

"I've had a pole and flung a line in the Berkshire rivers. Nothing more than that."

"Catch anything?"

"A trout or two. Not much."

"No trout here. We focus on cod caught by line from dories or in beach seines. Care to see how it works?"

"Of course. Ready and eager."

William and Ebenezer tie their horses to posts near the main building. George leads them over to the docks.

"This is the stage where the boat crews unload the daily catch."

Ebenezer watches men dump barrels of fish on the docks. Other men cut them open, pull out the entrails, rinse the carcasses clean in sea water, and then stack the cleaned fish on wood trays.

"The cleaning process goes on most of the morning when there's a good haul. We're a bit on the light side today so we'll finish this step in an hour or so."

"Why is it a light day?" William asks.

George shrugs. "You never know what to expect. I figure the storms on the horizon pushed fish deep, but I don't know exactly. If that's so, things will pick up. Nothing to worry about."

"I've heard talk in Halifax that these waters are fished out," Ebenezer says. "Might that be why?"

"I don't know about that. Seems to change by the day. Time will tell, I suppose."

The Captain says, "Show us the drying process, George."

George leads them away from the stage to some rows of open tables. "These are the flakes where we salt and dry the fish. We use a hard cure so the fish will stand up to export to England or ports in the Caribbean."

"How long do the cured fish last?" Ebenezer asks.

"Can be months, both in the warehouse and onboard the ships. The steps are simple. The salt draws out the moisture. Air drying leaves them hard as boards. Then they're loaded into barrels until shipment."

George leads them inside the largest of the frame buildings. Rows of large barrels fill the room. Straw covers the floor.

"This is where we keep the salted cod until it's time for shipment. The straw soaks up any remaining moisture. You'll notice the large open doors at both ends. They help circulate the air, which helps keep the fish dry."

"I take it that's critical, keeping them dry."

"Moisture is our biggest enemy. Soggy cod goes bad real quick. No smell worse than that."

"Have methods changed during the time you've been here?"

"We've moved away from line fishing to beach nets. That brings in a much bigger haul."

"Well, it's all very impressive. Anything else I should know?"

"Nothing comes to mind."

"I'd like Ebenezer to see the mill, too," Captain Grant says. "Can you take some time and ride over there with him?"

"I'd be glad to."

William turns to Ebenezer. "You don't mind, do you? I have some work to attend to in town. After you finish, we can meet for lunch at Foster's Tavern."

George and Ebenezer ride back to the mainland, then head north. Ebenezer asks about the labor employed by the Captain.

"Well, that's a long story."

"I've got time."

"It goes back a long way, to when we first came here from New York in 1783. We were part of a large evacuation from Manhattan. Local loyalists and soldiers. Black slaves from the south freed by the British for their service to the Crown during the War."

George waves his arm toward the town.

"A group of soldiers received land grants here. And about two hundred or so black men and women came here too as part of the Evacuation."

Ebenezer looks back to the buildings they had visited. George continues.

"When the Captain started the fishery, we employed freed black slaves. They were a big help at the fishery, until news of the new black colony in Sierra Leone came to Guysborough. Many of the blacks who settled here were fed up with cold winters, poor housing, poverty, disrespect. They were free, but wasn't this nearly as bad as slavery? At least that's how some thought."

George shook his head.

"That feeling spread throughout the community. Even among those working at the mill and the fishery. Although their lot was much better than most. They were ripe pickings when David George and John Clarkson came through. Reverend George stirred souls with the Bible. And Mr.

Clarkson, an abolitionist, offered farmland and warm weather and good jobs. He said they were creating a new black paradise on the coast of Africa. Many left then, and we were pretty shorthanded for a while."

"Were you tempted to leave too?"

"Maybe tempted. Who wouldn't be? The promise of sunny days on a warm beach. Unfettered and alive. One hand waving free, the other holding the hand of a lovely lady as we dance with soft sand between our toes. They painted a pretty picture indeed."

They reach a fork in the path. George leads them toward the sawmill and continues his story.

"We stayed, Lily and me. I guess that's obvious. Our situation was better than most blacks. Because of our connection with Grant. We had comfortable lives in Nova Scotia, unlike most of the other blacks. Still if I was tempted, Lily wasn't, so we stayed behind."

"And that left you shorthanded?"

"For a time, yes. But then we had another wave of immigration by the Black Maroons from Jamaica to Halifax in 1796. Some of them ended up here and worked with us for a time. But they too shipped out to Sierra Leone after a few years. It seems there was a rebellion there by the first wave of Nova Scotia settlers. So, the Maroons came in to put down the rebels.

"After the Maroons left, we brought on more men to keep up. Some freed black men from the Southern colonies who stayed here. Some young locals like Abijah Scott, a young boy still in school, whose family came to Nova Scotia before the War. And some of the local Mic'maq, when they're willing to leave the forests. It's quite a mix."

"Is it hard to find men?"

"Not too hard. Captain pays a good wage, so we've grown to one of the biggest fisheries—maybe the biggest—east of Halifax."

William reads the Halifax Gazette at a back table in the tavern dining room. Ebenezer arrives. William waves him over.

"I imagine you'd welcome a tankard."

"I would."

Ebenezer takes a seat at the table and a waiter approaches.

Grant points to his drink. "Make that two."

"How was the tour?" William asks.

"I quite enjoyed it. We had a nice ride, lovely setting, learned lots."

"He's a good man."

"He thinks quite highly of you."

"He would say that, whether true or not."

"I found him quite sincere. I take it you've been together a long time. How did you meet?"

"We met in Philadelphia during the War. I was ready to marry my first wife, Martha, and thought I needed a manservant. Many of the officers traveled with one, a privilege of rank. My inquires among them led me to George."

"How old was he?"

"Not yet twenty, but he spoke well, knew how to read, we got along well."

"Was he a former slave?"

"Heavens no. A freeman, born free. His family was from Africa, but never enslaved, and neither was he. His parents owned a music school, of all things. Taught the children of well-off Quakers to play piano, sing, read music, things like that. They also performed, as did George. He's quite good on the horn. But he was restless."

"None of that sounds like qualifications for a manservant."

"You're right. Truth is, he knew nothing useful at the time, but I liked him and gave him a chance. He rose to the task. I brought him along to New York when we stationed there. And then when we evacuated."

"How did he get along with former slaves?"

"Very well, though there was some tension when we got to Nova Scotia."

"How so?"

"He worked for me on salary, and I set him up with a house in town. Most of his kind who came over had no jobs when they arrived here, and no one to be their patron. They had to get by on their own, which was hard for many, too hard."

"What happened?"

"A combination of things—lack of paid work, tough farming conditions, demeaning treatment, harsh weather—all those things up against tales of a better life in Sierra Leone. The Evacuation ships from New York arrived here with over two hundred freed slaves. Within ten years, only half or less were still here.

"But he stayed."

Grant nods and takes another swallow of ale.

"He says he owes you a great deal," Ebenezer says.

"I'm glad he thinks so. But he has earned his pay and helps me tremendously. We've gone through a lot together. I'd say we're almost like friends."

Chapter Sixteen

William returns from the sawmill after sunset. Submit nurses Baby Elizabeth in the dining room. Mary gathers china plates and silverware from the imported mahogany sideboard. The smell of rosemary and garlic and the clatter of pots signal Lily's preparation of dinner in the kitchen.

William removes his boots by the fire and tells Submit about his day with Ebenezer. He thinks he will be a big help.

"What is he like?" Submit asks.

"I'll bring him to dinner. Soon, so you can meet him for yourself."

"Where is he from?" Submit pretends to listen, but focuses most of her attention on feeding Elizabeth.

"He works in Boston," William says. "But spends much time in Halifax. He's arranging a shipment of lumber from the mill and fish from the curing house back to Boston. He has clients in Massachusetts and is paying in advance for the goods. This is good for us. Quite good. It opens a new market. Most of our goods have been going to England. We will still do that, but Ebenezer will handle the shipments to Boston. It is an excellent arrangement. We are thinking of—"

He stops. Submit doesn't notice.

But Mary notices. She looks up when her father pauses and turns her attention to him.

"That's good news, father. May I get you something before dinner? A whiskey.?"

Submit enters the kitchen with new plans for Friday dinner. Lily stands in the center of the room and kneads dough on a worktable hewn from a pine tree cut near Grant's sawmill. Behind her are shelves on the walls cut from the same tree and an iron stove shipped overseas from Bristol. French copper pots and pans hang on hooks from the ceiling. A stock pot boils on the stove. Submit tells Lily that Captain Grant is bringing Mr. Partridge to dinner at the end of the week.

"We should serve something nice," she says. "A lamb roast. Or quail. Roasted potatoes. Fish soup to start."

"I'll go to the market," Lily says. "Will he be alone?"

"Yes, I expect so. Though Father may come too. We should plan for that. Let's feed the children early. The men will drink whiskey first, of course."

"Of course."

"Let's have the children finish their dinner before they arrive. Mary can help serve."

Lily says nothing, as if she knows this is not a good idea.

On the night of the dinner, William arrives home from work after dusk accompanied by a younger man. He looks to be in his late thirties. Fit, handsome, a bold smile. His thick dark hair swirls back behind his ears and curls over his collar.

Submit and Lily step forward to greet them.

"Mrs. Grant," William says. "Allow me the pleasure of introducing our new colleague, Mr. Ebenezer Partridge." Their guest offers his hand. Submit places hers on his and curtsies like a debutante accepting an invitation to dance a Viennese waltz.

"The pleasure is all mine," Ebenezer says.

"And this is Lily, the master of our kitchen. George's wife."

Ebenezer nods.

"May I take your hat, sir?" Lily asks. "And your cloak?"

"I hear you're a marvelous cook, Lily. I'm looking forward to learning that for myself."

"Let's settle into my study while we wait," William says. "I'm enjoying a tasty whiskey. It arrived this week with a shipment of supplies from Liverpool."

"Ladies," Ebenezer says, with a bow, and follows Grant into the other room.

Submit watches the men exit, then follows Lily into the kitchen. Lily hangs the guest's hat and coat on a peg by the wood stove.

"What do you think?" Submit asks.

"I have nothing to say," Lily says.

"Polite," Submit says.

"Yes," Lily answers, but she does not sound convinced.

"Easy on the eyes," Submit says.

Lily remains stoic.

Submit laughs. "There's nothing wrong with noting the truth," she says.

"If you say so."

The men enjoy glasses of whiskey in the study while they discuss business. Soon Submit comes to the door and invites them to dinner.

William rises, unlocks a cabinet, and removes two bottles. "This is my special occasion claret," he says. "

"I'm honored," Ebenezer says. "There could be trade in this."

"A smart merchant might make it so," William says, patting Ebenezer on the back.

They take their seats at the table. William at the head. Submit to his left. Ebenezer to his right. Lily pours wine. Mary sets a serving platter of roasted potatoes and lamb in front of her father. He fills a plate, then passes it to Ebenezer, exchanging his full one for Ebenezer's empty plate. He repeats this for Submit. William starts the conversation.

"Mrs. Grant, I believe you recall Mr. Stalton."

"Of course, we sailed with him from Guilford to Guysborough after the War. I was quite young then, but I remember him."

William pats her hand. "You're still young, my dear." He glances at Ebenezer and winks.

"I bring it up because Mr. Partridge tells me he is acquainted with him in Halifax."

"Indeed I am." Ebenezer explains he met Stalton arranging shipments from Halifax to Boston.

After a brief annoyance at her husband's remark, she shifts her interest to Mr. Partridge. He smiles when he talks, unlike William who usually looks stiff and stern. This seems remarkable. She wants to observe more. Submit has no interest in William's story about Mr. Stalton. When a pause allows, she asks Ebenezer about his family, hoping to see his smile return.

He tells her that he came from the Western wilderness, near Middleton, Massachusetts.

"What did you do in the War?" she asks.

"I was too young to do much of anything. And we were far removed and out of touch. Since then, I've lived on the road, wherever I have business, Boston, Halifax, Springfield."

"What is your trade?"

"Furs from the west destined for London. Textiles to take back to Boston and beyond in return."

"And now we are to add lumber and fish to the list," William says. "He'll be our agent to create a market for our goods in America. There's need for them in America. They're slow to welcome the return of the loyalists but quick to take our goods, if it's what they want."

Submit changes the subject. "Do you still have family in the west?" she asks.

"My mother died there. And I haven't seen my father since the War."

Mary Grant, clearing plates, speaks up, to William's surprise. "Do you know the Scotts?" she asks. "They are from the west."

"The West is a big place," William says.

Ebenezer turns his smile on Mary.

"I don't think we knew them in the West," he says. "But here I have met a young man."

"Abijah?"

"Yes, I met him at your father's mill."

Mary catches her father's eye and returns her focus to her task. She takes dishes back to the kitchen.

"She's a curious girl," Ebenezer says. "I don't mean odd. I mean inquisitive."

"Full of questions. And imagination," Submit says. "The other day at dusk she came in and said she saw a ghost. Imagine."

"Perhaps she did." Ebenezer shares his smile once again.

Submit searches his eyes for his meaning. *Did what?* Imagine a ghost, or see one? There is a charming ambiguity to Mr. Partridge.

After dessert, William leaves Submit and Ebenezer alone in the dining room while he goes to search the cellar for a special port. Ebenezer helps Submit clear the dishes.

"The Captain is a lucky man," he says standing close.

"Lucky about many things, I think," Submit says.

"Lucky about you." Ebenezer bushes her arm as he reaches for an empty plate.

William returns with a dusty bottle.

"Ebenezer, shall we?" He nods toward the study.

"Of course, Sir."

Submit does not expect an invitation to join them and none is extended.

"I will leave you alone, gentlemen. Mr. Partridge, thank you for gracing us with your presence. It was a pleasure."

"All mine, I'm sure. Thank you for the lovely dinner." He begins to extend his hand, as if he doesn't know that he should.

She does not reach for it. Instead, she curtsies again. Then looks toward William. "Good night, my dear."

Once the men are seated in the study, William pushes the port forward.

"I think you'll enjoy this," he says. "Carleton gave it to me in New York, before the evacuation. He was handing them out. He said, 'Gentlemen, if we can't hold Jefferson's country, at least we can hold his port.' He claimed it was seized from Monticello at the start of the rebellion. Which would make it close to thirty years old at this point. Or more depending on when he—Jefferson—procured it."

"Very special indeed I'd say."

William pours. The men toast.

"To our success," William says.

"And confusion to our foes," Ebenezer says. They drink and savor.

"Quite nice," Ebenezer says. "And quite a story."

"A good story, indeed, but not true, of course."

"No?"

"Soldiers are like fishermen, my friend. There may be a grain of truth to it, but the stories soldiers tell about war always exaggerate."

"I suppose that is true of most men," Ebenezer says.

William raises his glass in knowing agreement.

When they finish, William pours more. They discuss their plans to sell lumber in Massachusetts.

"I suppose you may have to keep the source secret," William says. "I doubt the rebels will want to do business with a British soldier."

"It's been a long time," Ebenezer says. "Many of the merchants, like me, were only children then. And memories fade."

"Not memories of war," William says. "These days we hear about the battles between soldiers but forget about the citizens. It was a time that broke apart families. Separated men who did not bear arms. The Franklin family, for example. Old Benjamin siding with the rebels and his son, the governor of New Jersey, going with the Loyalists. One nearly crowned king of the colonies. The other in exile in England. Their bonds of love turning to bitter hatred. And that's but one example. There are many in Boston who will have nothing to do with a loyal British soldier like me. Hell, the Adamses still hold sway in Boston. I wouldn't set foot there for fear of being tarred and feathered in the street by sanctimonious Puritans."

William downs the rest of his glass and lifts the bottle. Ebenezer waves him off by lifting his half full glass.

"I'll end with this," he says.

William fills his own glass.

"I dare say, it was good to have you here for dinner. Mrs. Grant has been so absorbed in being a new mother. Although she had become a mother to my other children, this was the first of her own. There must be a special bond there. Stronger even than the bond between man and wife. It was good to have you here, to break the routine."

"I enjoyed it and am grateful to you for having me."

"How did you find our humble home?"

"Quite wonderful. Very spacious, very warm, comfortable."

"No grand hall or manor, of course, not really, but we are content."

"It was an excellent dinner."

William nods and takes another gulp of port.

"And what did you think of my wife, my young wife, Submit?" He peers at Ebenezer with raised eyebrows.

"I found her to be quite gracious and hospitable." Ebenezer chooses his words with care. "You are a lucky man."

"Having company here did her good. She was quite engaged. More than I've seen for some time. Animated even. Energized. Not like I've seen her in ages. It was a balm to have company. I fear she must be quite bored with me."

William's gaze drifts off. His mood has changed.

Ebenezer says nothing, as if waiting for something more. William only stares down at his near empty glass, then reaches for the bottle to refill it.

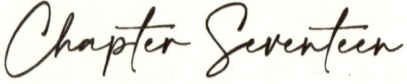

An hour later, William enters the bedroom. Submit is in bed. Her eyes are closed when William comes in, but she hears him. He stumbles against a chair. Submit opens her eyes but does not speak.

"May I join you, Mrs. Grant?"

She says nothing. He removes his clothes down to his underclothes. He asks her about the evening. His speech is slurred.

"Did you enjoy the dinner? You seemed quite taken with Mr. Partridge. Quite an attractive man. And young. Strong. No doubt virile." He slides into bed next to Submit. "Do you imagine yourself with someone like him? Young and strong and virile?"

She turns away in bed, but he presses against her.

"Not an old goat like me," he says, "but a young buck." He presses against her harder. She can feel the firmness of his erection. "Do you imagine him like this?"

"Stop saying that," she says. "You've had too much to drink."

"Just enough," he says and pulls up her nightgown to expose her bare buttocks.

"Please, not now," she says. But he does not stop. He pushes down his underpants and rubs himself against her backside. He forces his hand between her legs and rubs her there. She does not resist. She does not react either. She submits.

"You belong to me," he says, "old goat or not." He presses himself inside her.

The next day, Mary uses the pretext of shopping in town for buttons and thread for a rendezvous with Abijah. She sneaks up from behind and greets him with a flirtatious tap on the shoulder farthest from her. She laughs a bit too much when he looks the wrong way.

Before he has a chance to react, she launches into a litany of questions. She's been saving up.

"I need to speak with you." She pulls him into a vacant doorway.

"I'm listening."

She holds him close. "What do you think of Mr. Partridge? You've worked with him. What do you think?"

He shrugs. "Not sure. He gets on well with your father I'll say that."

"But how do you feel?"

"I shouldn't say."

"You must."

"You won't tell on me?"

"No."

Abijah leans closer. "I don't trust him."

"Why?"

"I don't know. He talks with you about you and your family. How people in the town get on. How things are with your father and with Mr. Leete. He listens and learns lots but says very little about himself. He says nothing about his home or his family."

"Maybe he has nothing to say."

"Maybe. Or maybe he has something to hide."

Mary thinks more about this. He came to Guysborough from Halifax, didn't he? "Maybe he's a pirate," she says.

The long days of summer pass. There is a thickening in her belly and Submit discovers she is pregnant again. She finds comfort in this. It keeps William from molesting her at night, although he is moody from the inattention.

His moodiness increases after baby James is born. He spends long hours at work, much of it with Ebenezer, who now runs their shipping operations.

One evening after dinner, Submit is alone in her bedroom nursing the baby. William stands in the doorway watching for a few moments.

"I will be leaving soon for London," he says. "I have business there, some new opportunities to exchange salted cod for cloth."

"Lily told me."

"I worry about you and the children. I will be away for more than a month."

"We'll be fine." She and Lily already manage fine every day as it is. "My parents are near if we need anything."

"Your father has not been well lately, as you know. I don't want to trouble him while I'm away. Or your mother." He moves near and strokes the thin hair on the baby's head.

"I want to be sure you and the children are safe. Ebenezer will manage the business while I'm away, and I've asked him to watch out for you. He agreed. And knowing he is coming by to check on you will ease my mind." He caresses her cheek and smiles.

This news dumbfounds her. She thinks of Ebenezer often, ever since he first came to dinner last spring. But she has avoided being alone with him. She last saw him at the Leete's New Year's Party when he kissed her hand to celebrate the start of another year. She has thoughts about that kiss most nights as she lies in bed waiting for sleep to arrive. Does William know this? Is this plan for her protection a test? What is he thinking?

Part Five

1804

Chapter Eighteen

ary Grant stands on Guysborough Dock with Submit and
Ebenezer. They bid farewell to her father as he begins his journey
to London.

"Come here my darling."

He stoops to give his daughter a bear hug. She's unhappy to have him
leave, but savors his embrace. It is a crisp, cold morning. She feels warm in
his arms.

Her father marches to the end of the dock. He salutes, then turns back
to board the sloop that will take him to a larger ship in Halifax for the long
sail to London.

Submit stands close to Ebenezer, cuddles her baby with one arm, and
waves to William. This angers Mary. Submit and Ebenezer look like a
married couple waving goodbye to the child's grandfather. Mary clenches
her jaw and hurries away. Ebenezer offers a ride back to Grant Hall in his
carriage, but she declines. She'd rather be alone with her thoughts. With
Isobel dead and John at the garrison in Halifax, she feels a duty to protect
the Grant family, the real family, the family as it existed before Submit's

intrusion. And what about Ebenezer? Like Abijah, she doesn't trust him. He's too charming. Smiles too much. He should not be standing in her father's boots. Why can't he take Submit away, and the baby too? That would be perfect.

Over the next fortnight, Mary watches Ebenezer with the attention of a hawk eyeing a field mouse. She doesn't like what she sees and angles to discuss what she thinks with Abijah. They agree to meet outside the general store after his classes.

He's waiting for her when she arrives. She leads him to the end of the municipal dock where they can talk without being overheard.

"I know Ebenezer has promised to take care of Submit and the family while Father is away. But he takes his responsibility too seriously."

"What do you mean?"

"He often comes by on horse for breakfast. Then he works during the day and comes back for dinner in the evening."

"You do that at our house. I wish you'd come more often."

She ignores him and continues, "He and Submit sit in the parlor afterwards and talk. I watch them when I pass by or when I can find an excuse to come in the room, to get a book or something."

"What do you see?"

"Nothing. They just sit and talk."

"Do they look guilty when you interrupt them?"

"No, they're as natural as can be. That's the problem."

"What do they say?"

"I hear nothing specific that they say. But I hear laughter. Often."

"And that worries you?"

"Yes, Submit seems happy. I can't remember her being happy before. At least not since she moved in."

"She has a new baby. Maybe that makes her happy."

"It should, of course. But her husband is away. She should not be happy."

"She makes the most of it."

"She makes too much of it. She has a child and is sitting with a charming man her age who could be her husband. But he is not."

"So that's what angers you?"

"It doesn't seem right." She turns away, walks toward the river, and hesitates. Then she twists her head around to look back at him.

"I will tell you what it is. What I really think. I don't want either of them around, happy or not, but it's worse when they're happy."

"So, what will you do?"

"I will watch. I will wait. I will find something to drive them apart."

Abijah looks away toward the ocean.

"I know what you're thinking," she says.

"What?"

"That this is none of my concern and I should leave them alone."

"Yes, I am thinking that. But I know you won't." He pulls her close and wraps his arms around her.

That night, Ebenezer is still in the parlor with Submit when Mary goes up to bed.

Mary spends as much time as possible in the arms of Abijah, and now that she's sixteen more intimate thoughts arise in her vivid imagination. That night those thoughts become more disturbing. In her dream, she and

Abijah have escaped from the rain into a covered doorway. Her white blouse is soaked, translucent, the buds of her breasts visible beneath the wet cloth. He leans in to caress her. But then the dream shifts to Submit and Ebenezer. Together in bed. Naked beneath a thin white sheet.

When she wakes in the morning, she looks outside at a brilliant March day. Ebenezer's horse stands in the courtyard, hitched to a post.

She finds Ebenezer in the kitchen with Lily, drinking coffee.

"You are here so early." She recalls the vision of him in bed with Submit and blushes.

"Yes, I woke early and had a lovely ride at sun-up."

Mary doesn't believe this. It is too much of a piece with her dream. She turns toward Lily. Will she confirm that this is true? But Lily's placid face reveals nothing.

But Mary can't dismiss it as nothing. At least she must investigate.

And so, she heads outside. A late winter day. The cold wind makes her eyes water. She checks on Ebenezer's horse. If Ebenezer had been riding, the horse should be warm, sweaty. But it is cold. Isn't this the proof she needs, confirmation that he lied and spent the night, as she saw in her dream?

Chapter Nineteen

William returns in mid-March. The family celebrates his return with a feast to rival Christmas. He has presents for them all. Toys for the younger children. Dresses for the women. The trip was a success. He secured new customers and vendors for the business Ebenezer is helping him grow. After dinner, he finishes a bottle of the wine he's brought back, cites the weariness of travel, and goes up to bed early.

The next morning, he asks Mary to join him in his study, where he unpacks and organizes the papers from his trip.

"How were things while I was away?" he asks. "Was Mr. Partridge attentive?"

"He was very attentive, Father."

"Good."

"Too attentive."

"How so?"

"Here almost every day, morning and night."

"Was Submit happy?"

"She was very happy."

"Did she miss me?

Mary begins to cry.

"What's wrong?"

She blubbers through her tears. "She is in love."

"I know. Of course she is. She has a new child."

"No, it's not that. She's in love with Ebenezer, I know it."

This is all she can bear. She runs from the room in tears.

William finds Mary in the family parlor, sitting at the harpsichord, staring at a page of sheet music.

"What do you know? What did you see?" His voice is insistent, tense, the voice of restrained fury.

Mary tells him what she saw and felt—Ebenezer drinking coffee in the kitchen, the cold horse hitched to a post.

He eases at her story. It's not conclusive. An early morning ride proves nothing. He goes about his business the rest of the day and returns home for dinner.

The scene seems normal. Submit holds the new baby. Lily serves dinner. The children play upstairs. But, the thought of his wife and Ebenezer together in bed at night gnaws at him. After dinner, alone in his study with a bottle of whiskey, he thinks of little else. Why was Ebenezer there so much? And into the evening? That is not what he expected. Or is it? Was he a fool to create the opportunity for this to happen? How can he know? If Mary is right, surely Submit and Ebenezer would deny such betrayal.

He wants witnesses. The younger children might know. He could quiz young William, but he likes Ebenezer. They go riding together. He will have only good things to say about him and would be oblivious to the dynamics of a man and a woman left alone.

Lily probably knows the truth. She returns home to George every night after her work, but she would still know if a man had slept the night. If the couple had sex. There would be evidence in the morning when she cleaned Submit's room. The whiskey bottle is nearly empty when he decides to press her for the truth.

He stops at the open kitchen door. Lily peels potatoes at the kitchen table and watches him enter. His gait is clumsy. He's been drinking. She has seen him like this often. He'll be short-tempered. He'll say things he doesn't mean and seem to remember none of it the next day.

He stands opposite the table a few moments before speaking. When he does, his words are deliberate yet slurred.

"Did Submit spend much time with Mr. Partridge while I was away? Mary says he was here every day."

She continues to peel.

"You wanted him to come, you asked him to, to be sure Submit was safe. I heard you say so before you left."

He steps around the table.

"Did he stay the night? Mary says he did. I certainly didn't ask him to do that."

He steps close to her. She smells whiskey on his breath. She turns away to set the bowl of peeled potatoes in the sink.

"I do not stay here for the night. How would I know if he were here?"

"You could tell in the morning. Was he here when you arrived?"

She does not answer. She had served the Grants for many years. But, she never felt part of the family until Submit arrived. They have grown close. Her loyalty lies with her.

"Your silence confesses the truth," he says.

She faces away from him. He clutches her shoulders. His body touches her backside.

"Did he have his way with her?" His voice is rising. His words are clipped and fast.

She remains silent. She remains still.

"Like this?"

He presses hard against her from behind and grabs her breasts.

She pushes him away, spins back to the table, and lunges at the knife she left on the pile of potato peelings.

Grant grabs her arm before she reaches it. She loses her balance, hits her head on the edge of the table, and crashes to the floor. Blood spills from a cut on the side of her head.

Grant's voice softens. "Lily, Lily, I'm sorry." He stoops and reaches for her.

She pushes him away leaving blood on the front of his shirt. "Don't touch me."

He says her name again.

She says nothing more, pulls a dishcloth from her belt, and presses it against her bleeding head.

He mumbles. "I didn't mean—I—I—" His words become gibberish and he leaves the room.

Chapter Twenty

George lies in bed awake with Lily next to him turned away to face the wall. He wants to touch her, reach out and comfort her, but does not want to disturb her sleep. She would not say how she injured herself, but he is confident that Grant was responsible. This is not the first time.

He heads to work before sunrise to ready the fishery. The first boats will land soon with the overnight catch. This is also where the boats of negroes left for Sierra Leone.

If only they had gone with the others when they had the chance. Lily would be free from Grant's mistreatment. And he would not be tormented as he is now by his loyalty to Grant and his anger at him for disrespecting his wife.

At breakfast the day after their confrontation, William acts as if nothing happened. Lily hides her head wound with her bonnet.

When Submit enters the dining room with the baby in her arms, William looks up from his broadsheet, as usual. Lily carries in a fresh pot of coffee. Submit greets them both, and William helps her with a chair.

"Good morning, Mrs. Grant. I hope you slept well."

"James slept the night. That was a blessing. But I heard noises. Banging from outside. I reached for you, but you were gone."

"Raccoons. I heard them too. From the study."

"Working."

"Thinking."

"About what?"

Lily sets a plate of warm toast and a cup of fresh coffee in front of Submit, who thanks her with a smile. Lily's nod is almost imperceptible as she turns and leaves the room.

"It's good to be home," William says. "To see you with the baby, to hear the raccoons at night, to smell clean sea air instead of the tainted Thames. I'm sorry I was gone so long."

"Will you leave us again soon?"

"Do you want me to?" His smile suggests he's jesting, but it seems that something unspoken is on his mind.

"No, of course not. But will you?"

"There's need to get back to London soon, but I've decided to send Mr. Partridge instead. That is what I've been thinking about."

"When?" Did that sound too eager? Why should she care enough to sound so demanding? She regroups.

"I hope you won't work too hard while he's away. The children and I are selfish and want you to ourselves."

William looks pleased at this. "Soon. A few weeks from now. As soon as we can get organized to fulfill the orders coming in from London. I plan to speak with him about it today when he returns from Halifax." He reaches out to clasp her hand so that it nests like a small bird in his palm. "It would be nice for us to have some time together, alone, don't you think?"

Submit smiles and nods. She hopes William will read this as obedient consent and not detect her uncertainty.

"I asked Lily to bring lunch to the mill today. Could you do that instead? It's a lovely day for it."

"Of course. That sounds nice. I'll have Mary watch the children. I could use a break."

The sun is high in the sky when Submit arrives at the mill. Her wicker basket is full. Fresh bread, cold sliced ham, soft sheep's cheese, pickled cucumber, and a bottle of cold sweet tea. She hears sawing before she smells the sawdust in the air, the toasty, acidic smell of fresh cut pine. Inside George guides a spruce log against a large circular saw. Abijah stands nearby and helps balance the cut boards. George pauses when she enters, nods a greeting and says something. But the high-pitched sound of the metal blade against wood drowns out his voice. Submit waves a greeting and Abijah points toward Captain Grant's office at the back of the mill.

William greets her with a kiss on the cheek and leads her back to a table on the loading dock. He takes the basket and inspects the contents.

"Wonderful! Fit for a king."

Submit is glad that he approves. He helps her spread a tablecloth and unpack the basket. They settle in at the table and take their first sips of tea.

"I'm glad we can have this time together," he says, after swallowing a bite of bread smeared with cheese. "I've been wanting to find some time alone with you. To talk."

"About what?"

"I wonder how things went while I was away. How you all managed."

"We were fine. We missed you, of course, but we managed. Mary was a big help with the children. I am grateful for that."

"And Mr. Partridge? What of him?"

"We were glad for his attention. He came by from time to time. Even went riding with young William."

"From time to time?"

"Yes. Most days probably. The children like him. So does Lily, I think, though it's hard to know what she thinks most of the time."

"And you? Do you like him?"

"Well enough. He's pleasant company and helpful. We felt safer having him come by."

"Mary says he came to visit every day. She says he spent the night."

"I think so. There was a storm one night, so he slept in the guest room."

"Only one night?"

"Perhaps another time. I'm not sure." Submit wonders what more she should say. What does he know? What did Mary tell him? What did Lily say?

His eyes meet hers as if searching for clues that would betray a darker truth. She cannot maintain his gaze and looks away.

"I want you to understand this," he says. "That I understand. He's a young attractive man. It would be natural for you to have feelings for him. Fond feelings. But—"

"Don't go any further with that thought." Submit says. "He is your protégé and I treat him so, nothing more." She reaches for his hand, which he surrenders to her. "You are my husband and the father of my children. That is all that matters to me."

Her mother would be pleased. It is indeed all that should matter.

She can hold his gaze now. He is the first to look down. He lifts her hand, brings his lips to it, and kisses her wrist. It feels like the brush of a feather.

"That is all I can ask for," he says.

Chapter Twenty—One

A week later, Submit is in her bedroom, nursing James. The baby sucks and gasps for air until satisfied, then nods off to sleep with his cheek resting on Submit's bare breast. She dozes too, until stirred by the sound of a horse rushing up to the house and Ebenezer's insistent voice.

"Help. Help!"

She rushes downstairs with the baby and joins Lily and Mary on the front porch with Ebenezer.

"What is it?" she demands.

Ebenezer comes near. "There's been an accident at the mill. Captain Grant—."

"What happened?"

"An accident. He's dead."

"Take me there."

"You shouldn't go." He reaches his arms out to hold her, to pull her close while she still clutches baby James. "It's terrible. He fell against the saw. There's blood everywhere. Like a battle scene. You don't want to see him like that."

Submit freezes in place as if time is standing still. She now sees the blood stains on Ebenezer's shirt and jacket.

"This can't be true," Mary yells. "Who did it?"

"I don't know. No one. He was alone, on the floor bleeding when I arrived. I tried to help but it was too late."

"Was he still alive?" Mary asks.

"Yes, but not long. I was holding him when he died."

"Did he speak?" Mary demands. "What did he say? Tell me."

"He was still alive for only a few moments. I heard him say 'take care of her.' That is all. Those were his last words."

"I can't believe this. How could you leave him alone?" Mary bolts from the porch and runs down the hill toward the mill.

Ebenezer shouts for her to stop but she keeps running. He moves to go after her but Submit holds him back. "Let her go," she says.

William is not dead yet. He lies wounded on the sawmill floor and sees himself again at the Battle of Bunker Hill.

He rides forward flanked by the grenadiers of his Scottish regiment.

As he nears the rebel battle line, he is engulfed in the acrid smell of burning powder, the rattle of ramrods shoving home another volley, the whiz of cannonballs that miss, and the terrible thud of balls hitting home.

Bullets strike mounted officers on either side of him. A colonel to his left in the thigh. A captain on his right in the arm. His new hat is blown off his head and two balls rip through his coat. His horse throws him to the ground, leaps a fence, and gallops into the rebel lines.

An approaching soldier's head vanishes in a crimson mist. His own uniform is splattered with wedges of tissue, dislodged teeth, and skull fragments. He tries to wipe away the blood and brains with a handful of fresh dirt, but the effort is futile.

British reinforcements charge up the hill. The explosion of firearms becomes a continual sheet of lightning and incessant thunder. The advancing soldiers fall like grass when mowed.

All goes blank.

Mary arrives at the Mill, out of breath. Her father lies on the floor, his left side facing toward her.

"Father." Her voice is soft, little more than an exhale, as if she's trying to wake him from a nap. "Father, please, say something. It's me. Open your eyes. Please."

She lifts his head and feels his damp, sticky skin. The right side of his face is slashed open, his ear and part of his cheek torn away, and a deep gash cuts into his shoulder. The floorboards around him are tacky with coagulating gore. She collapses onto him with her head pressing against his chest. Her tears mingling with his blood.

Then Abijah calls to her. She lifts her head and looks toward the voice. Abijah stands in the doorway, silhouetted by the afternoon sun behind him.

"Mary, what happened?"

She says nothing. He rushes to her side. "My God, my God, my God," he says, and pulls her into his arms.

Chapter Twenty—Two

April 14, 1804.

Dear Mary,

I am so sorry for your loss, and in such a tragic and sudden way. My father is so old and I never thought you might lose yours before I lost mine. I feel guilty. Not that I had anything to do with it, of course. But because you've lost both of your parents and I still have both of mine. You have Submit, but I know that's not the same for you, as you've told me many times. I just wish you could see her the same way I do. You might find some comfort from her. I know you must be thinking — how could he die like that? Perhaps there's no answer. You have a right to feel moody and blue. I do, too. I feel that way for you now. When I was younger and felt that way, Submit would give me a hug. Perhaps she'll give you one now. I hope so.

Your friend forever,

Huldah

Much of the town files into Christ Church for Captain Grant's funeral. Reverend De La Roche stands at the pulpit facing the crowded pews. The soldiers of the 22nd Regiment, Captain Grant's old unit, stand at attention around the nave's edges, dressed in their formal uniforms - red coats, buckskin breeches, and black tri-pointed hats. All except for John Grant, now a member of his father's regiment. He sits with his siblings in the front pew, facing a closed casket.

The Grant family fills the front row of the church. Mary and her siblings sit on one side. Submit and her parents on the other. The newest member of the family, baby James, sleeps in Submit's arms. Sarah holds Elizabeth, not yet two, on her lap. Huldah sits beside Andrew Leete.

Submit turns her head toward Huldah, who leans forward to look toward Mary Grant. Submit follows Huldah's gaze. Mary stares back, her lips tight, her eyes dry. What do these girls think? On the threshold of married life, soon to have husbands of their own, who may die, and leave them widows like her? Mary has lost both her parents in a few short years. Does she suffer a greater pain?

I cannot know her pain. But I know her anger. She despises me. What can I do? Respond in kind? Let a child control my feelings, what I do, who I am? I am the widow, not yet thirty, left alone with a house full of children. How will I manage? I have no space in that for concern about Mary's anger.

James squirms in her arms. She looks forward at the casket. He said he understood. She will miss him. He was a good man for the most part, distant but usually kind. Even so, there is relief in his death, the freedom of a bird released from a cage.

Leave Mary to her anger, fly from it, do not let it become another cage.

The Reverend's voice pours over the congregation.

"Behold, I tell you a mystery; we will not all sleep, but we will all be changed, in a moment, in the twinkling of an eye, at the last trumpet."

He lectures on about the mystery of death, and the importance of faith in the afterlife.

What about the mystery of now?

If I am free now to enter that uncertainty, what will I find?

William's final words return—*take care of her.* She turns away from the casket, back toward the pew where Ebenezer sits, head bowed, as if in prayer.

Chapter Twenty-Three

After the funeral, Magistrate James Hart walks north on Church Street. He turns down Pleasant Street at Foster's Tavern toward the waterfront. He turns again at Main Street and walks north until he reaches the courthouse, next to Alexander Torrey, Carriage Maker. Seagulls squawk and soar overhead against a clear blue sky. Moored boats bounce on gentle waves in the harbor. Loosely furled sails flap against tall masts.

Hart enters the courthouse, a two-story building built with boards from Captain Grant's sawmill, where the floorboards are still stained with blood. Although the sun is bright outside, the light in the office he enters on the ground floor is dim. He opens the shutters, lights a whale oil lamp on a wooden desk, and reaches his hand toward a honeycomb of storage nooks filled with rolls of parchment tied with crimson ribbons.

He spreads out a clean sheet on the desk, dips a quill in ink, and writes:

"Summons, dated April 17, 1804, for the inquest into the causes and circumstances of the death of Captain William Grant, issued by the undersigned, duly appointed by his Majesty King George III,

Whereas Captain Grant died on April 12, 1804, from injuries to his head and body originating from uncertain causes, we deem it necessary and appropriate to commission an investigation involving interviews of various and diverse persons who may have information relevant to those causes, to be initiated as soon as practicable by the appropriate officers of the Colony of Nova Scotia."

A fortnight later, the daily packet ship from Halifax arrives mid-afternoon. It carries official dispatches, business mail, packaged goods, and a few passengers. One of them is Chief Constable Charles Gardner, a big man wearing a waxed gilet and a canvas duster wet with sea mist. He carries a leather bag and has a pistol and cutlass belted to his waist. He hails a harbor boy to carry his bag and walk him to his lodgings at Foster's Tavern. The quotidian sights and sounds of a prosperous village grab his attention. A black dog digging in a yard beside the road. An elderly woman pinning wet laundry on a line. Boys chasing after a ball in the middle of the street. He hears the clop of horses' hooves on Main Street's cobbles and smells fresh pie cooling on a bakery's windowsill.

Inside the tavern, Constable Gardner collects his room key and note from Magistrate Hart. Once settled, he wanders over to the Christ Church cemetery. He takes slow deliberate steps down rows of grave markers noting the names of families. He pauses at the grave of Captain William Grant.

"Who killed you, Captain?' he says. "I wish you could say."

The next morning, Constable Gardner waits at a table by the front window of the Tavern. The signs of morning pass by. A waitress serves him breakfast: fried eggs and potatoes with slices of fresh bread. He unfolds the pages of notes sent to him by Magistrate Hart and adds his own notations in the margin with a stub of graphite inside a wooden stick:

Motive? Widow, Partner, Negro, Merchant?

Opportunity? Merchant, others?

Alibi?

Accident?

He rolls up the papers and stuffs them in his leather bag, finishes his eggs, and leaves the tavern.

Inside the courthouse, Constable Gardner takes a chair beside Magistrate Hart's desk. The morning sunlight pierces into the room and illuminates floating dust motes. A lamp burns on the desk. The smell of stale fish fills the room. The Magistrate pours each a cup of coffee.

"What about the widow?" Gardner asks.

"Young, pretty, pleasant to visit with," Hart says.

Gardner scowls. "Did she do it?"

Hart shrugs. "She was home at the time according to the housemaid."

"You always wonder about the widow," Gardner says. "Especially the young ones."

"Not this time."

"What about the merchant? I gather he's a stranger here."

"He's the one who found him dead. I wouldn't think the murderer would report the death. Besides, he's a Mason."

"Evil surprises us all."

"Mr. Leete vouches for him, says he and Grant were on the best of terms, building up the business together."

"That might be a reason. Take over the business. Or the widow if she's as pleasant and comely as you say."

"I don't see it. He doesn't act like a guilty man. More like a man who's lost an old friend."

"What about Mr. Leete then?"

"Too old. He wouldn't be able to overcome a man like Grant."

"All right. When can we talk to his servant? George, is it?"

"He should be here soon."

It is after dark by the time Lily gets back to her house from Grant Hall at the end of her workday. George stands is standing in their small parlor. On the floor is a wooden trunk, covered with deer hide, held shut by forged iron locks.

Lily hangs her bonnet on a peg by the door and steps forward. She reaches up and touches his cheek.

"How did it go?" she asks.

"I don't know."

"Who was there?"

"Only Mr. Hart, and a constable from Halifax named Gardner."

"What did they ask?"

"Everything. How long I'd known Captain Grant. What I did for him. What I thought of him. Things like that. And then they asked me to describe what happened the day he died. They asked for a lot of details. Where I was before it happened. Who I was with. Why I went to the mill.

What I saw. What I did. Then it seemed like we were done, and we started talking about fishing. But at the last minute when I was ready to leave, they told me to come back after lunch. And so, I did. And they asked me the same questions again about the day he died."

"It's easy for an honest man to tell the same story twice. Hard for a liar."

"I said what I had to say, pretty much the same both times."

"Did you tell them you were at the fishery when it happened?"

"I did."

"How did that go?"

"They wanted to know who was there. I told them it was only the crew from the fishing boat, no one from around here."

Lily looks down and pushes the trunk with the toe of her shoe. "They must have believed you. Otherwise, you wouldn't be here."

"They asked how they could find the crew. I said I didn't know them. I said they headed out as soon as they unloaded, headed to Labrador. The Constable laughed at that, and said 'invisible men aren't much of an alibi, are they?' Hart got a good laugh out of that, too."

Lily purses her lips and nods her head. "Put that way, I'm worried. What do you think?"

"They were tough men to read. I'm worried too. I can't tell if they are suspicious about anyone else or not."

"What about Partridge?"

"They asked about him. I said I didn't know much about him, that he was new here. But look, he's a white man, a Mason, wears nice clothes. I'm a Negro, a working man. Who do you think they're going to blame for this?"

"So, what's next?" She looks down again at the trunk.

"There's a sloop headed to Halifax first thing tomorrow. I can get the ship to Sierra Leone from there in a day or so, like we said."

She embraces him, hugs him tight, buries her face against his neck.

"They'll chase after you."

"Not right away. I heard the Constable say he was heading to Dorchester before going back to Halifax. It should be days or even weeks before they know I'm gone."

"They'll come talk to me about this."

"And you will say what we've been saying. We've been planning this for years. I've been wanting to go ever since we heard of a better life in Africa, but didn't because I was loyal to the Captain. Now that he's dead, there was nothing holding me back."

"What if they never ask?"

"Either way, I'll send for you once I get settled."

"What about Submit, this is so sudden?"

"I told Ebenezer after the funeral that I planned to go now that the Captain was gone. He wished me well."

Lily starts to cry. George kisses her forehead and strokes the hair on the back of her head as he whispers in her ear, "We'll be alright."

The next day the Constable and the Magistrate sit near a window at the Tavern, order lunch, and discuss their morning interviews.

"So where are we?" the Magistrate asks. "We haven't talked to the widow."

"No need, like you said before."

"And George?"

"Can't see it. He'd been with the Captain for more than twenty years, owed him for a good life, a house, better job than most. Loyal as can be, and grateful. He'd be more likely to give his life to save the Captain than take it."

Foster sets plates of lamb stew and two tankards of ale on the table.

They wait for him to retreat, then the Magistrate asks, "What next?"

The Constable lifts his ale and smiles. "I'd say we're done. Sometimes an accident is only an accident."

Chapter Twenty—Four

Mary Grant sets the table in the dining room for the children's lunch. The front door slams. Her brother John bulls into the room. He's dressed in full uniform, ready to charge enemy lines with sword raised.

Mary sets down stack of plates and step toward him.

"What's wrong, John? What is it?"

"Is she here?"

"Who?"

"Her. The weeping widow."

The disdain and sarcasm in his voice surprise her. She has never seen him like this before.

"She's gone to visit her mother, gone with baby James in the carriage. Less than an hour ago."

John scowls, lurches forward and leans against the table, head bowed.

"I've come from a meeting with Andrew Leete. Now that the inquest is over it's time to settle Father's will. Leete showed me the papers Father signed before he married her. They change everything. Nothing that I—

that we—expected will come to pass. Father has left us nothing, almost nothing."

"What do you mean?"

"Everything changed when he married Submit. I will not inherit the businesses or the estate. There's an addendum we didn't know about." John pulls a folded stack of papers from his coat pocket and throws it on the table.

"This. This pile of—this says she inherits the house and the property. Her father takes over the businesses for her until she marries. Then full ownership passes to her husband. I receive a small income from the rental of land for farming and some of father's military memorabilia." The consonants burst from his lips with disdain. "A pittance and a pile of puke."

He hunches forward with his arms clutching his chest. Every muscle in his face pulls tight. And then he releases the tension with a heavy sigh. Mary doesn't know what to do. What to say.

John settles onto a dining chair. "I am told," he says, his voice now soft and weak, "It is my Father's will that I make my own way in the military." He taps the papers on the table with his index finger. "And you and the other children. This says your stepmother will care for you as if you were her own. That is what this says. *As if you were her own.*"

"Oh, John. What will you do?"

"I don't know. But there must be a way. A way to break this. In court. Or some other way. To get even."

When John has left, his words still echo in her mind. She needs air, the smell of pine, the movement of her feet, to grasp what she has learned.

Before she had suspicions, now she has proof. Ebenezer has a motive. He had the opportunity. If he marries Submit, all will be his. The inquest may be over, but they are wrong, it wasn't an accident.

She rushes down the hill from the house to the waterfront. *I must stop this, stop them from getting married, but how? I have no proof.*

The mill is not far off. Closer by than Abijah's house. The mill closed after her father's death. Before that, Abijah usually worked there in the afternoon. She has not seen him since the funeral but she'll look there first. She needs him now, to confide in, to test her theory, to help her.

As she approaches the mill, she notices that all is quiet. No sound from the saw. And the air is clear. No smell of fresh cut pine. She enters the mill. No one is there. She approaches the place where she found her father and cradled his mangled head. The floor is still stained with his blood. She feels bile rise in her throat. She needs air, or she will vomit.

Outside, on the loading dock, cool clear spring air brings relief. There, she finds Abijah, alone at their picnic spot, facing the river flowing to the estuary.

She calls his name. He raises to embrace her. She presses her forehead against his neck. They stay like this for several moments. Then he leans back so he can see her eyes.

"You look scared," he says.

"I need to tell you something," she says. "I know what happened, Abijah. I know they murdered my father. And I know why."

He leads to sit at the edge of the dock, and the words flow from her. She connects all the thoughts and emotions and beliefs that make up her theory.

"But I don't know what to do."

"Come with me," Abijah says. "Let me show you what I found."

He walks her back into the mill. Off to one side he points into a dark corner.

"See this, an empty whiskey bottle. And this, a board, stained with something, it looks like blood."

He nudges the whiskey bottle with his foot, but leaves it in place.

"I haven't moved them," he says. "This is where I found them. Off to the side. Hidden. If your father died in an accident, how would a blood-stained board end up here?"

Mary hurries back to Grant Hall. She barges into the family parlor, where Submit is reads a worn copy of *Clarissa*.

"I need to speak with you," Mary says. "Now. It can't wait."

Submit closes the book.

"What is it? Is something wrong?"

Mary steps close to the chair where Submit sits.

"Yes, very wrong," she says.

"I'm listening."

"I know how Father died. It wasn't an accident. I had my suspicions, but now I have proof. It wasn't an accident."

"What was it?"

"Murder. And Ebenezer is the one who did it."

"Oh no, you poor thing. He wouldn't do that. How can you think that? He loved William like he loved his own father. And William loved him."

"I don't believe you."

"I'm afraid it doesn't matter what you believe. It's the truth. Whether you accept it or not is your affair."

Mary tells Submit about the board Abijah found inside the mill.

"If it was an accident, how did a bloody board end up hidden in a dark corner across the room?"

"That proves nothing."

"You only say that because you're involved. Weren't you? You both were in on it, weren't you? You both plotted to kill him, so you could get married and take over the businesses. I know about Father's will. And I know you were cheating on him while he was away. You both betrayed him."

Mary is screaming now. Her spittle splashes against Submit's face. Mary rants on until Submit stands and slaps her on her left cheek, hard, with an open hand.

"That's not true," she says, her voice calm and deliberate. "None of that is true. Don't ever think that, or say that, again."

Mary clasps one hand to her slapped face. Then, with her eyes wide with anger, she pushes Submit in the chest with her free hand. Submit loses her balance, falls backward against the side table, knocks it over. Mary runs from the room. Submit crumples on the floor, amidst shards of broken china and a puddle of tea.

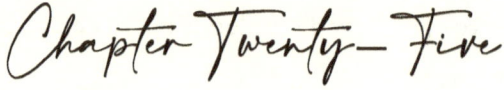

Chapter Twenty-Five

Submit, still wearing widow's weeds, sits William's desk in the study at Grant Hall, reviewing ledger books for the sawmill and fishery. Ebenezer enters and Submit rises to meet him.

She leads him by the hand to a settee near the large windows overlooking the estuary.

"How is Father?" she asks.

"He seems well, well enough for a man his age."

"And what did he say? About us?"

"He gave us his blessing, as you said he would."

"What did he say about the will?"

"He said he's recorded your interests. Once we're married, everything will be ours. He sees no problems with that.

"We need to talk more about that."

"You have doubts?"

"Conditions."

"I love you, Submit. I'll do anything you want."

This will be new, a surprise, they have not talked about it before. She has given it much thought and decides to soften the message.

"I love you, too, Ebenezer. I want you beside me every night. I want your name." She pulls his hand to her belly. "I want my children—our children, this child—to have your name."

"I want that too."

"So, we must get married soon."

"As soon as you say."

"But before that, I need you to agree."

He clasps her hands in his. "To what?"

"You must agree that we will be equal in all things. I will be your wife, but I will not be a servant or a silent partner, in life or in business. Especially in business. We will run the businesses together by equal and mutual consent."

She plants a kiss on the back of his hand and looks into his eyes.

"Those are my conditions. Do you agree?"

July 6, 1804

Dear Mary,

I know that you are shocked that Submit would marry Ebenezer so soon after your father's death. Not even three months later. There must be reasons unknown to either of us that will be revealed in the fullness of time. But you must wonder, what could the reasons be? Money. Love. A child? Their rush to the altar gives the impression that they are glad to have your father in the grave.

Whatever the reasons, though, I can't believe what you are thinking. What you meant when you said at the church after the wedding that you knew your father's death was not an accident. I wanted to press you on that but had no chance. You can't have meant that they caused his death. Submit would never be part of anything like that. You can't possibly believe such a thing. And you can't possibly believe such a thing about Ebenezer either.

But it's not just that you might think they had something to do with your father's death. More than that, it was the look in your eyes, the coldness, when you turned away from me. That you were turning against me in your heart as well. That you have tarred me with the resentment you have invented for them. What is this? Guilt by association? Guilt because I am her sister? Anger because I cannot think ill of them as you do? Anger because I accept that your father's death was an accident while you embrace the delusion that it was something else?

How can you reject me so? As I write these words, I know I will never give this letter to you. How could I? These private thoughts should go with me to the grave, remain unspoken, unread forever.

Perhaps one day we will get past this. I hope so. We are—were—best friends. But now I don't know.

In early autumn, Sarah and Huldah dine alone at Leete Manor. Sarah's hand trembles when she brings a spoonful of soup to her lips. A moment later she drops the spoon on the table, slumps in her chair and falls to the floor. Huldah rushes to her side, squats next to her and lifts her head. Sarah opens her eyes.

"You fainted, mother," Huldah says. "Let me help you up."

Sarah remains in bed for days afterwards, unable to stand. Andrew sits beside her for hours, holding her hand. When he tires, Huldah or one of the other daughters watches over her, feeds her, reads the Bible to her.

October 4, 1804

Dearest Submit,

Mother died tonight, a few hours after you left. Father was sleeping when she passed. I was with her at the time, seated beside her bed, reading from the Psalms. I paused and she said in a whisper, "I am very happy." Then I sensed her soul leave, and then she was gone with her body left behind. I wish you had been there with me at the time. I needed to hold your hand. To collapse into your comforting embrace. To wipe my tears on your shoulder. To hear you say everything will be alright.

I am sad for all of us at her passing. But I am saddest for Father. We are alone now, the two of us, the oldest and the youngest, in this big sad house filled with her spirit. I'm not sure he can bear it. He has become so frail, and this will age him even more. Please sit with him at the funeral and hold his hand. I know that will be a comfort.

With love, your sister, Huldah

Submit enters the churchyard cemetery. The grass drips with morning dew. She places a bouquet of flowers on her mother's grave near the plots for the Grant family—Rebecca, William, Isobel. A chill runs up her back, a premonition of many more in time. She rubs her hand over her pregnant belly. Another young child to join the ones left behind by Martha's death and the two she herself bore for William.

That leaves her with the youngest children—Barbara, Donald, their young half-sister Elizabeth, and baby James, not yet a year old—all in her care. Young William is ready for boarding school and will soon be gone. And then there's Mary. She could be a help if she ever overcomes her grief and bitterness at her father's death. What chance of that?

Thank you God for a big house and Lily's help. How would I manage otherwise?

Part Six

1805

Chapter Twenty-Six

Mary stands beside Abijah in the Christ Church graveyard. Abijah reads the name from a new gravestone.

"Abigail Partridge. No day or month of birth or death. Only the year and the name."

"It is a sign of God's wrath," Mary says. "For the evil they have done. For Father's death. And John's. For all they have done, they are cursed with the death of their child."

"But John died at sea," Abijah says. "On route to Gibraltar. Surely, they can't be blamed for that."

"I can blame them for everything. As God surely has."

She lays a small bouquet of flowers on the grave. "This poor child, alive only five days, conceived in sin before their marriage. Her death, proof of their evil."

"At the funeral, Ebenezer said the baby was born too soon, in a rush to get to heaven."

"Yes, Submit told me the baby was premature, unable to survive birth. But I saw her, no smaller than any other baby newly born."

Abijah reaches for her arm.

"I fear you make too much of this."

She stiffens at these words and turns to him.

"I do not. I make exactly as much of this as should be made."

"What would you do about it?"

"Destroy them, destroy their marriage, destroy their lives. Make them suffer the way I have suffered. All of that would be too little."

Abijah takes her into his arms and looks down at Abigail's grave.

"Isn't this enough?"

Mary says nothing and stares at the new grave, with only one thought arising in her mind.

No, this is not enough, they still have each other, and that is too much to bear.

Abijah wipes a tear from her cheek.

"Let's think of other things," he says, as if he knows her thoughts. "Let's think of us. Let that be enough. Let me make that enough."

She leans in and rests her head on his shoulder.

I hope you can, Abijah, please try.

Lily rides a carriage into town to buy supplies and passes by the harbor. The packet boat from Halifax bobs beside the dock. It's fittings clang against the mast with the rise and fall of the water.

At the General Store the clerk tells her a man from the boat came in that morning with a delivery for her.

"He tried to find you at your old house," he says, "but learned you didn't live there anymore. So, he came here. I offered to keep the package here, but the man said he had to deliver it himself to where you live. I told him that you've moved up to Grant Hall. I hope that was alright."

Lily goes back to Grant Hall. Submit greets her at the door.

"A man came by a short time after you left asking about you. He said he had a delivery and wanted to know if you lived here. He looked respectable—well dressed, polite—so I had him put it in the dining room."

Lily finds the delivery on the dining room table. It's the wooden crate that George took with him on his trip to Sierra Leone. Could it be the message she's been waiting for, that he's sending for her to join him in Africa?

Inside the crate are some of George's clothes and an envelope sealed with wax. The letter is from a magistrate in Sierra Leone.

"Dear Madam, I regret to inform you—"

She drops the letter on the floor, looks up toward heaven, covers her eyes, and shouts, "No."

Submit hears Lily's cry and rushes to the room. Lily slumps forward with her elbows on the table. Her face presses against the palms of her hands. Her head shakes from side to side. Submit sits beside her, rests her hand on her shoulder and feels her gasp for air. Lily turns her way. They fall into a tight embrace with Lily's damp face against Submit's neck.

Chapter Twenty—Seven

April 1, 1805

Dearest Submit,

I can't wait to tell you my exciting news. Father told me this morning that he is taking me to London for my seventeenth birthday. It is time for me to meet society, he says. What fun! He says he feels well, and he seems stronger these days. I worried that the trip might be too much for him, but he says don't be silly. He says it will give us something to look forward to and help us both get over Mother's death. I wish you could go with us.

Love, Huldah

June 8, 1805

Dearest Submit,

I received your birthday wishes last week but have been so busy since that I only now have time to write. Father and I had a most wonderful time in London, but my birthday was extraordinary.

We stayed for a time with Aunt Emily in Dodington. I had with me the book you gave me years ago, the one by Mary Wollstonecraft, about the rights of women. I was reading it one morning. Aunt Emily noticed and told me the most extraordinary thing. She said she was quite friendly with Mrs. Wollstonecraft's widowed husband, William Godwin, and offered to make an introduction. Anyway, I convinced Father to write as we were headed for London to celebrate my birthday. Remarkably, Mr. Godwin invited us to call.

We had a most wonderful visit. Mr. Godwin was raising his daughter Mary, a precocious young girl, only eight years old. He believes the ideas of his late wife and gives his daughter an excellent education. I have not met anyone as young who seemed to know so much, to be so intelligent for her age.

When I asked what she wanted to be when she grew up, she promptly said "I want to be a paleontologist." Can you imagine? That from an eight-year-old! And the way she said it, I sure she will if she decides to. Her attitude was so modern, I thought, so in keeping with her mother's work on the rights of women. I trust she will do great things one day.

I said this to Mr. Godwin and he inquired about my knowledge of his wife's work. We had a wonderful chat in which I bragged about you. Father bragged about you too. I hope you don't mind. Mr. Godwin seemed quite impressed to learn that you were running the businesses of Captain Grant after his death. I told him that you were the person who gave me his wife's book. He said we both might enjoy his recent book about her life. He left the room and brought back a copy of "Memoirs of the Author of a Vindication of the Rights of Women," which he presented to me as a birthday gift. He inscribed it, "To Huldah, A Living Vindication of Mary's

Philosophy." Isn't that the most extraordinary thing? Can you imagine that happening to a girl from Guysborough?

I've started the book and it's fascinating and a bit scandalous. I will share it with you when I return. That won't be for quite a while though. Father is returning at the end of the month. But he's arranged for me to stay longer with relatives of Aunt Emily. I can spend more time exploring the museums of London, see theater, hear concerts. I so look forward to this.

Thank you very much for remembering my birthday,

Your loving sister, always,

Huldah

June 18, 1805

Dearest Submit,

I'm quite moved by Mr. Godwin's memoir of his wife.

He writes, "Independence was the object after which she thirsted." That seems so bold and reminds me of you. I see that arising in you since the death of Captain Grant.

Mr. Godwin also writes about his wife's concern for her younger sisters. She thought it would be "respectable and agreeable" for them to become "governesses in private families." She therefore determined "to endeavor to qualify them for such an undertaking" by securing an education for them.

What do you think about that for me?

I could become a governess, or maybe a teacher. Do you suppose father would find that "respectable and agreeable"? It would mean of course that I would stay in Europe longer than planned.

I would find that very agreeable. Tell me what you think.

Your loving sister,

Huldah

September 10, 1805

Dearest Submit,

You will have heard from Father about my alleged misconduct — he calls it a betrayal. He says he trusted me in the care of friends and family in London, and I betrayed his trust. It is all a huge misunderstanding, but he refuses to listen.

I left with our cousin Claire on our journey believing she had the blessing of her father, although it was later revealed that she did not. But Father will not believe my innocence. He writes that my claimed naivete is unbelievable, laughable even, more amusing than true, if it weren't so sad and disingenuous.

Perhaps, if I can explain myself here, you can intervene, and he will believe you and forgive me and trust me again.

Before Father returned home last spring, I lodged with Aunt Emily's brother-in-law, Sir Everett Dodds, a widower, and Lord of Doddingham Manor, as a companion to his daughter, our cousin Claire Dodds.

We became fast friends, and she soon invited me on a European tour. She said her father was funding the trip and that he approved if I would go too.

I'll grant you, the idea of a sixteen-year-old chaperoned by a seventeen-year-old does seem, in retrospect, to be far-fetched, but at the time I was so taken by her excitement and my own desire to see Europe, that I gave the absurdity of the plan little thought. I had by then read Mary Wollstonecraft's report of her travels in Europe and the romantic appeal of such travel was irresistible. I wanted to believe — and therefore did — that her father approved.

While Uncle Everett was away on business, we left on our journey, first sailing across the Channel to Calais, where we were greeted by Nigel Witherspoon, who Claire called her fiancé. I was of course surprised by this, but his charm won me over and I was relieved to have a male traveling companion for our journey. There is safety in numbers, after all.

We made our way to Paris by coach where we stayed for several days with Nigel. We then resolved to walk through France. Each day we entered a new town and found affordable lodgings. This continued until Claire sprained her ankle. At that point we hired a carriage and traveled to Geneva to visit another friend of Nigel's. We spent some time there, boating on Lac Leman, hiking in the mountains, feasting in the garden, and amusing ourselves late into the night by reading ghost stories seated around a log fire.

It was a wonderful trip—the chance to speak refined French, see the history of the Church through its cathedrals, discuss literature with knowledgeable friends, see the collection of Fine Art amassed in the Louvre, listen to live symphonies and operas performed by skilled musicians—I learned so much, and there was so much more to learn and see and feel.

Unfortunately, money ran low, so we moved on to the Rhine, where we caught a riverboat back to the North Sea, returning to England, parting ways with Nigel, and returning to Mary's home in London. That is when I discovered with shock that Claire's father knew nothing of our trip. More to the point, I discovered that I was blamed for the whole idea. But surely you can see that I was an innocent in the matter.

If you love me, and I know you do, you will please convince father that I have done nothing wrong.

Your loving sister,

Huldah

October 1, 1805

Dearest Submit,

Thank you for intervening on my behalf with Father. He has found me a position as tutor with a family in Glasgow, which will allow me to stay in Britain for another year or so. I'm sure your kind words softened his hard heart.

The situation is quite suitable to my skills and interests. I will have my own room. There are two young children in the household—twins—both girls. I am to teach them to read and write. The family will spend most of the year in Scotland, but relocate to Nice in the winter, so I am also expected to teach the children French. That ability at least is a benefit of living beside the Acadians in Nova Scotia most of my life.

With love,

Huldah

December 15, 1805

Dearest Submit,

I long to share with you this unbearable sadness I feel, knowing that you too have known it, and only now appreciating what you know from that feeling of ultimate loss - the loss of a child so shortly after she enters this painful world. I bear this in secret, fearing I can tell no one, fearing I could not withstand the embarrassment, if the fact is known that I have miscarried the child I conceived last summer in a moment of youthful passion. To make matters worse, I disappeared from my post as tutor before my condition could be detected. I have told no one where I am and you all must now wonder what has become of me, am I alive, where do I live, how do I live?

I wish I could write you and answer these questions, but—

Chapter Twenty-Eight

Huldah sits alone on a bench in a park in London, her head bowed. After a few moments she takes a white handkerchief from her handbag and wipes her eyes.

Fallen leaves rustle nearby and she looks up. A man wearing a long black coat and a top hat stands a few yards away. He smokes a clay pipe. He pulls a slip of paper from his coat pocket and brings it to the smoking embers of his pipe. Puffs of smoke drift up and a red glow illuminates his face. In a moment the slip of paper catches flame. He holds it up by a corner and lets it turn to ash. When he let's go, it floats off with the afternoon breeze.

The sight of the man in black casting ashes to the wind triggers a shudder of sadness within her.

The man turns her way. She looks down, again wiping her damp cheeks with her handkerchief.

He approaches.

"Excuse me, Miss. May I assist you with anything?"

He removes his hat revealing a bald head, a smooth face, soft wrinkles around his eyes.

"No, I'll be fine. I'm sorry, I shouldn't be like this in public."

He smiles and nods.

"May I sit with you?"

She pauses a moment, then motions to the empty place on the bench beside her.

He sits, rests his hands on his lap, says nothing. His kind face and calm manner sooth her.

"Spring will be here soon," she says, not knowing how else to deal with his silence.

"The cherry blossoms here are lovely," he says.

"I haven't had the pleasure."

"You are a traveler?"

"Yes, for some time now."

"Your accent tells me you may be from America."

"Canada. Nova Scotia, actually. And you?"

"Born here, but I have lived in Japan for many years and only recently returned."

A flock of pigeons approaches and lands nearby. He reaches into his pocket, pulls out a handful of seeds, and tosses them near the birds.

"They know me," he says. "I come here as often as I'm able. I always bring something."

The birds squabble and peck.

"I'm happy to listen, if you'd like to tell me why you were crying."

"Oh dear. That's kind, but I don't want to burden you with my troubles."

"No burden." He tosses more seed at the birds.

"I was thinking about my sister's daughter. The baby died soon after she was born. Thinking about that triggers my sadness." A pang of guilt stabs her heart when she says these words. Guilt because she cannot voice the full cause of her sadness, the loss of her own child.

He turns up the collar of his coat.

"It's still a bit chilly. Would you like a cup of tea? There's a place nearby. Excellent tea from China."

He stands and offers his hand.

She hesitates.

"My aunt said I should avoid tea houses, that they are not a proper place for a lady. Perhaps she is just being old fashioned."

"Not at all, but this is not an ordinary tea house. It's a private house where the niece of Lord Dorchester hosts tea."

"*The* Lord Dorchester?"

"Yes, the former Governor of Canada."

"I come from a village named for him."

He smiles.

"What a coincidence. I'm sure your aunt would approve."

She accepts his hand.

"Yes, I suppose she would."

They walk a short way and enter a lovely townhouse. A servant greets them and shows them to a back parlor overlooking a garden. They take seats at a small table by the window.

Huldah's escort turns to the servant who is ready for their order.

"Oolong, please," he says.

They exchange names. He is Michael Cavendish. She asks about his travels to Japan.

"Such an exotic place, I imagine," she says. "So distant."

"Yes, in so many ways." He explains that he was the third son of a minor lord. His eldest brother inherited the title. His next brother is a London barrister. So, he, of course, became a minister.

The tea service is brought to their table, and Cavendish continues.

"I entered the Church because it was the thing for the third son to do. Either that or the military or medicine, which did not appeal to me. I'm afraid I had no real calling for religion, but I was a bookish sort. I became fascinated with Japan at University and decided to find out for myself. One brief trip led to many more. At one point I even studied to be a Shinto monk."

He pours the tea and offers her a slice of lemon.

"I found the traditions quite interesting. Their rituals regarding death, for example, might interest you."

Huldah sips her hot tea.

"Please tell me more."

"It is common to be in mourning for forty-nine days after the funeral," he says. "Each week the family will visit the grave to leave fresh flowers and burn incense. The graves are very important. Usually a stone monument with places set aside for flowers, incense, and water. All this shows high esteem for the deceased and brings great comfort to the bereaved."

Huldah nods. She has not properly mourned her dead family—her mother, Submit's daughter, her own child, who remains unmentioned, a secret held close to her heart.

"Perhaps that is what I need," she says. "A better means to mourn the loss I feel."

"Yes, perhaps it would help."

"May I ask about something else?"

"Of course."

"What were you doing before you walked over to me. I saw you burn a piece of paper."

"A ritual of my own. Inspired by another Shinto practice. In Japan it is common for the faithful to leave prayers and wishes at a Shinto temple on small wooden plaques called ema tablets. Later the priests burn the plaques sending the wishes and prayers to the gods. I've created my own version with my pipe and pieces of paper."

"What do the faithful wish for?"

"Many things - health, wealth, a large family, a good crop."

"And you?"

"Me? I wish to be forgiven." He pours each more tea. "What would you wish for?"

Huldah looks out at the garden.

"I think I would wish for bad memories to be forgotten."

That night, she mulls over the day spent with Mr. Cavendish and the Shinto rituals they continued to discuss on their long walk after tea.

And then she dreams. She's in a grove of trees, the place where she buried the small remains of her dead child. She kneels beside the stone that marks the spot and lays fresh flowers on the ground. She lights a stick of incense and plants it in the ground with the flowers. There is no name or date on the stone. Nothing.

Part Seven

1808

Chapter Twenty–Nine

March 15, 1808

Dearest Submit,

Cousin Claire forwarded your sad letter, which reached me today. I am devastated by the news of Father's declining health, and have decided to return immediately, or at least as soon as transportation can be arranged. Tell him I will be there as soon as I am able.

I am sure you will be most surprised to receive this from me after my long silence. It is a long story I may tell you in person one day. Until then, I want you to know I am fine. I have been working as a teacher in Geneva for the past year, living a simple comfortable life.

I yearn to see you soon!

Your loving sister,

Huldah

Huldah holds her father's penis and guides its tip to the opening of a clay jar. A few drops of urine dribble out, no more than a thimble full.

"Is there more, Father?"

"I feel the need, but cannot execute the task, my dear. That must be all for now." He leans back against the pile of feather pillows behind him, exhausted.

"Will you eat something?"

He shakes his head. "Perhaps some water," he says.

She places a small wet sponge on his lips. He sighs, then drifts off to sleep.

She reads by candlelight about the final days of Christ in the Book of Matthew while her father sleeps.

Then he stirs.

"Huldah. Huldah. Are you here?"

"Yes, Father," she reaches for his hand.

"Can you forgive me?" he asks, with a breathy voice that is only a faint whisper.

"For what, Father?"

"For my sins."

"I know of none to forgive."

"I have treated you unfairly."

"Never."

"I have, in many ways. And I have committed other unforgivable sins in secret. Mortal sins."

"Surely not, Father."

"God knows the truth."

"He will forgive you."

"I know he will not unless I confess before I die."

She listens as he strains to disclose the deeds that burden his soul, the blood that has stained his hands, the secrets he has kept. She struggles to hear. His voice is a whisper. She only understands part of what he says.

Finally, with a firm voice, he says, "You must never tell anyone about these things, this is for only you and God to know, do you promise?"

"Of course, Father."

He closes his eyes with relief and says, "May God save us both." He chokes on the last word, coughs. She hears the air rattle in his chest as he sucks in a last gasp of air. His grip on her hand goes slack. And all is silent.

Huldah stands at the crest of a hill near Grant Manor and stares out to sea. Submit calls out her name, and Huldah turns. Submit approaches with papers in her hand.

"You should read this," she says. "It is his will. His final will, delivered to the house today by his lawyer."

Huldah reads through the short statement of her father's final wishes. She then walks away to a nearby bench, sits and reads the will again.

"I don't understand, who is this son he mentions, Jared, what son?"

Submit sits beside her.

"His first-born son," Submit says. "By his first wife."

Huldah shakes her head.

"I can't believe this. I never heard of a first wife or this son. Why have I never heard this?"

"We left that life behind when we came here."

"So you knew?"

"I was young when we left Connecticut, only thirteen, but I remember."

"What did you know?"

"He was part of the family, a good bit older, independent, but he spent much time with us. I was told Father had been married before, but that his first wife had died, so Jared lived with him. Mother was Father's second wife but raised Jared as her own."

"Why wasn't I told."

"There's a dark side to this, that I didn't know about until later when I found some court papers in his study."

"What happened to them? Those papers?"

"I'm not sure. It was years ago. He often burned old papers in the fireplace. I forgot about them until now."

"What do you remember?"

"Father's first marriage didn't end because his wife died. He got a divorce because she deserted him for another man. They had one child before that, Jared, the son mentioned in the will. Father raised him on his own, until he met our mother. She had also married before and had a daughter named Cassandra." Submit points to another line in the will. "Mother's first husband was a sailor who disappeared at sea, so she was also granted a divorce."

"I see nothing wrong with any of that. Why keep it a secret?"

"It was a difficult time. The War was waging. Father wanted to stay neutral. He thought the colonists should stay loyal to the Crown and work things out. But Jared had different views. He joined the militia, fought against the British. The War divided them, and they were never reconciled. Things became unbearable for Father. He was even put in jail. I was only a young child then, but I remember. He said it was for no legitimate reason, only on suspicion. I remember him saying those words, but I didn't know what he meant."

Huldah thinks about her father's confession but holds back what she knows—that it was more than suspicion, because she promised to stay silent.

"Finally they let us leave the colony," Submit says. "Father sold his land—hundreds of acres—and we traveled here. Jared stayed behind, siding with the Patriots. Father felt betrayed and said he never wanted to speak or hear of him again. As far as I know, Father had not seen or heard from him since we left."

Huldah looks down, rereading the bequests.

"That explains his spite. He includes him—names him first even—but gives him five shillings only. Not even enough to buy a decent meal."

"I'm not surprised," Submit says. "Our father was a stubborn man and slow to forgive those who wronged him."

"But then why this? Why give Jared's son, who we've never met, who has never been here, a 200-acre farm and half of his entire moveable estate?"

Submit shakes her head.

"I have no answer. Perhaps he felt regret for not being there, for neglecting his role as a grandfather. His reasons lie with him in his grave."

Huldah tallies up the bequests to her siblings in her head—160 acres and a fine house for Andrew, 200 acres each for Jabez and Lucretia, and even more for Eunice. Her hands tremble holding the papers.

"What is it?" Submit asks.

"I can't understand what he was thinking. After giving away his property, he gives half of his moveable estate to an unknown grandson and the other half to Eunice. It is spiteful of me to think this way, I know, but why single her out for more?"

"She was his housekeeper in the years since Mother died. I suppose that is why."

"He gives you only 90 acres. Don't you feel that's unfair?"

"I married well. He knew that. I have more than enough."

"And then what of me? I was with him at the end, caring for him, keeping him clean, wiping sweat from his forehead, feeding him. And what does he leave me? Twenty acres of swamp and three pounds." She shakes her head and laughs. "At least it's more than he leaves his disloyal son."

"He made this will before you returned. Imagine what was in his mind."

"He knew it was unfair. He told me so. But I didn't know then that this is what he meant."

"When?"

"The day he died. He asked me to forgive him for treating me unfairly."

Submit nods her head and reaches out to touch her sister's arm.

"He also asked for forgiveness for his sins," Huldah says.

"Many do before they die."

"He said they were mortal sins that even God could not forgive." Huldah looks away into the distance. She wants to say more but holds back, determined to honor her promise. It would serve no useful purpose now to reveal his dying words.

Submit touches her arm.

"A man who lives as long as he lived is likely to amass many regrets. He went through complicated times—two marriages, the War, a life of business deals, of choosing sides, many things I know nothing about."

Huldah stares at the estuary, gathers her thoughts, appraises her emotions.

There must be another will. He must have changed his mind and left me something more. I'm not surprised, he never loved me the way he loved the others. But he took me to Europe, he set my life in motion. I'm the one to blame, of course. I chose my path. I was blind to my cousin's disobedience because that is what I wanted. If this is all there is for me, fine. I can make my own way.

She will put this behind her. There's more to life than her father's land and money. There's love, friendship, adventure, beauty, Fine Art. There's the man she left behind in Switzerland. The chalet on the hill, the dark room at night, guttering candle flames catching the evening breeze, the look in his eyes as he enters her.

Submit squeezes Huldah's hand.

"Are you well, sister?"

Huldah returns to the bench on the hill.

"There's nothing for me here," she says.

Chapter Thirty

May 28, 1809

Dearest Submit,

I hope this letter finds you well. As I write this I realize it's been a year since Father's passing. You will wonder what has happened to me, and I apologize for not writing sooner. After our talk on the hill about Father's will, I decided to return to Europe. I know my departure was abrupt. I packed my bags and left early that morning, saying goodbye to no one, not wanting to be questioned, not wanting to have my resolve weakened, not wanting to be stopped or followed.

I found a boat at dawn to Halifax, and from there boarded a ship to England. I found lodgings with a friend of our cousin's and made plans to move on to Geneva, where I had stayed on my famous misadventure. I will say, the planning was liberating, as I felt no familial limits—no mother, no father—to hold me back. No one to judge me, save you. But I know in my heart that you understand, and do not judge me.

I wrote Charles, my lover in Switzerland (see how easy it is for me now to write that? Are you proud of me?). He wrote back expressing much happiness to know I was near, or nearer at least. I wrote that I would be making my way to him as soon as possible without waiting for a response.

I arrived in a fortnight. He was surprised to see me. Embraced me awkwardly. Then took me inside to meet his visiting family and guests, including Alice, a beautiful young French woman, who he called his fiancée! He introduced me as his old friend. I found it hard to believe. I felt lost in a dream. I tried to speak with him privately, but he would have none of it. He was cold, cruel, spoke to me like I was a scullery maid. He said, "We amused ourselves then, nothing more." I left that same day before dinner holding back my tears, walking as far away as I could before nightfall. I slept that night on the ground in a field hidden from the road. Eventually I reached Zurich and found work as a tutor.

Since then, I have made my own way in the world, working now as the manager of a bookshop and giving private English lessons. I'm doing fine and am happy with my simple life. My job occupies the days, and friends, cafes, dancing, wine, and good food occupy the nights. I feel independent and free, like an unfettered colt full of life. I harbor no regrets.

Please send news. You are what I miss most.

Your loving sister,

Huldah

Chapter Thirty-One

May 29, 1809

Dearest Submit,

Even now I cannot tell you all. Even now I shade the truth, twist it, keep it to myself. I paint a rosy picture, but it is not true. You see, my lover—I will not say or write his name again—did not only speak to me like a scullery maid but treated me as such. It was violent, with no love at all.

A few months later I realized I was pregnant.

I became ill and could not do my job as a tutor. I was homeless and lost until some nuns took me in at their convent. They saved us both. My child, a boy, was beautiful, like a cherub. They took him away for adoption before I could think of a name.

He remains nameless in my mind, a fading memory, chubby, with blond curls.

My body was saved, but my soul is broken. And this is what I cannot tell you now. What I shall never tell. I will mail the other letter, but not this.

Never this.

Chapter Thirty-Two

Submit sits at William's desk, reviewing ledger books. She looks up when Lily enters the room. Lily takes a seat in front of the desk.

"We're all set," she says.

"And the food?"

"I finished the cake minutes ago. Have you heard anything from Ebenezer? Will he be back in time?"

"No, he won't. A letter came in this morning. He's delayed in Boston until next week."

"Nothing bad, I hope."

"Bad only because he's missing his son's first birthday. Other than that, the news is good. He says he's secured reliable new suppliers in Massachusetts for our fur trade. We're off to a good start, he says."

"It's a shame he needs to travel so much. It's been over a month since we last saw him. I miss him. The children miss him too."

"As do I. But we do all right, you and I, running things while he's away, don't we?"

Lily nods and smiles. "I wish George were still alive to see us now. I can only imagine what he would think."

"We've come a long way."

"And I thank you for that."

"No need for thanks. We're a team now, you and I. I couldn't do it without you, the children, the house, the businesses, it would all be too much."

"What are you working on?"

"You know the stones I've been collecting on the beaches most of my life."

"Yes, of course. I never understood why you kept so many."

"Turns out there's a market for some of them. We have a lot around here, but there are far more on the beaches up north. I'm looking into a plan to hire people up north to collect them for sale in England. The numbers look good. I'm eager to tell Ebenezer about it all when he gets back."

"More travel for him?"

"Of course."

"It will be nice when the boys are a bit older. They could help."

"Young William used to like beach rocks. I'd like to get him helping Ebenezer on his travels. So he learns the trade. If we take on minerals, on top of lumber, fish, and furs, we'll need more help."

"I don't suppose Mary—"

"No, I don't either. Her mind is elsewhere. I wish it were not, but it is. She blames Ebenezer and me for her father's death. You and I both know that."

"We see so little of her. She's always with Abijah, it seems."

"Thank God for that. I confess, it will be a relief when they marry and he takes her away."

Beneath crumpled sheets in a small cabin near the sawmill, Mary and Abijah separate. She turns her back to him and he holds her close.

"When do you leave?" she asks.

"Soon. Father hasn't set a date."

"How long will you—"

"We don't know. It's up to Father. He's the one that insists we go."

"I hope you won't be like this when we're married."

"How do you mean?"

"Like Ebenezer. Traveling all the time. Leaving me alone."

"I won't. We're visiting Father's family, that's all."

"How do you get there?"

"Boat to Boston, coach to Springfield."

"Where is that?"

"West. A long way west. It will take us days to get there."

She rolls back to face him. "You'd better not forget me."

"I couldn't if I tried."

"Or let any other girls do this." She runs her fingers from his neck down below his waist and strokes him back to firmness.

Mary gets up from Abijah's bed and walks naked over to the washbasin in the corner of the room. She soaks a hand towel in soapy water, wipes herself between her legs, and hopes this prevents her from becoming pregnant.

Abijah props himself up against a pillow.

"Come back to bed," he says.

"I need to leave."

"Why?"

"I told you. Submit is having a birthday party for Henry."

"Stay. He's only a year old, he won't know if you're there or not."

She stands before him and pulls on her undergarments.

"I wish I could." She leans forward and kisses him on his chest. "I don't look forward to it." She slides back into bed beside Abijah and strokes his belly.

Abijah starts to rub her between her legs, but she nudges his hand away.

"No more of that," she says, and rolls away from him laughing.

"Will Ebenezer be back?"

"Don't bring him up. Thinking about him makes me furious, you know that."

"Yes, I know."

"And you think I'm foolish."

"No. You have a right to your suspicions. And a right to be angry. He may have killed your father."

"He did."

"And he's taken your family's inheritance. I understand. I'm angry too."

"You are?"

"Of course. What angers you angers me."

"Really? Then I better go or we'll both be angry because I'll be late and inflicted with even more of Submit's disdain than usual."

Mary leaves Abijah, glad to have a moment alone.

He tries, but this doesn't make him angry the same way I am angry. He isn't sure about Father's death. But I am sure. But what can I do? I am angry about so much. Father's death. The theft of our family's fortune. Submit's happiness. This feeling that I am alone against the world. Only Abijah relieves that.

She walks the path leading from Abijah's cabin to Grant Hall. Soon she sees the big house ahead on the rise of the hill. The afternoon sun sets the facade aglow in yellow light. Lily and the younger children are arranging the settings on the tables in the front garden. The edges of white tablecloths flutter in a light breeze carrying the salty smell of the sea.

I wish I could feel part of that. Those children show sadness although they have lost both Mother and Father and Isobel and John in only the span of a few years. Do they still remember that? They must, but they live in the moment and in this moment are happy, without a care. They can't understand all that we have lost, and how we lost it. Lost it all through the treachery and villainy of Submit and Ebenezer, the very people they now call their mother and father. If I can find a way to destroy that marriage, do I bear the knowledge alone and do nothing? Or do I press on with the destruction even at the cost of disrupting their lives once again?

The truth must prevail, that above all. Even though they are young, they too must know the truth. And that is what she must pursue. Not revenge. Not recompense. But the truth no matter what.

Chapter Thirty-Three

Abijah has been gone close to a month. Mary sits on the front porch longing for his return. The children play tag on the lawn. The sun on her face feels warm and nurturing. The breeze coming in over the estuary keeps her cool. Young William beckons her to join in their games. She shakes her head, closes her eyes, leans back, and lifts her face to the sky. She is too old for children's games.

Lily interrupts her thoughts.

"A letter has arrived for you." Lily hands her the envelope and retreats inside the house.

A letter to her, in her name only. Her pulse speeds up. On the back she sees a wax seal and Abijah's name. She's relieved, the seal is still intact. Abijah's writing looks like hers, the same cursive style they learned as children, in bold black ink against thick white paper. She breaks the seal, unfolds the envelope and reads the letter inside.

Dear Mary,

I am writing this from Boston. We should be back in Guysborough by week's end. I miss you so and yearn for your touch and to tell you about our journey. Especially about our visit to my father's cousin in Middlefield. I told him stories about you, how we planned to marry, and how you lived with your stepparents and how your stepmother married a man named Ebenezer Partridge. He has a store in Middlefield and said he knew a woman name Rachel Partridge who comes to the store now and then and she was married to a man named Ebenezer, a merchant who is gone often, who returns from time to time, but mostly travels, so she's mostly left alone to care for her son. He said the man named Ebenezer is tall, good looking, with thick dark hair. He's in his mid-thirties. Doesn't he sound like someone we know?

That is enough for now, I will tell you more soon.

All my love always,

Abijah

Mary runs her fingers over the black letters, then rereads the description of the man named Ebenezer Partridge. Could this Ebenezer be her stepfather? Is it possible? Does Submit's husband have a second family? Is that why he is so mysterious about his past? And if so, what if Submit does not know? She can't know. She would never marry him if she did. And if she finds out, what then? It would destroy their marriage, wouldn't it. And that could destroy Ebenezer. Disgrace him beyond redemption. He could no longer show his face in Guysborough. He would not be dead, but almost so. This outcome is almost too wonderful to embrace.

Mary sips tea in the conservatory beside potted orchids. She tries to despise the flowers because Ebenezer brought them to the house. But they are too beautiful to hate. Ebenezer calls them vanilla bean orchids and that is how they smell. He says they are from Sierra Leone, a place settled by freed black slaves, the place where George died. There are ships now going back and forth from Halifax to Africa.

I wish he would take one.

Voyages to Africa can take months. Wouldn't that be nice if Ebenezer were gone that long?

Lily returns to the room, breaking Mary's reverie. She wears a fitted blue satin dress accented with contrasting velvet. A silver string with blue stones adorns her neck.

"Excusez-moi, mademoiselle, vous avez un visiteur, monsieur Scott."

Mary bolts from her chair.

"Oh, how wonderful."

She pulls her hair in place and considers her ordinary clothes. This is not the way she wishes to greet her lover who she has not seen for weeks.

"I must change," she says. "Tell him I'll be with him soon."

Lily smiles.

"Bien sur. Your new yellow dress is lovely, that and a splash of lavender might be well-received. I left a tincture from my latest batch by your wash basin."

Mary admires herself in the mirror. Lily is right, the new yellow dress hugs her close in all the flattering places. She hurries downstairs from her bedroom to the parlor. Her young siblings surround Abijah and pepper him with questions about his travels.

"Were there sea monsters?" her half-brother James asks.

Before he can answer, Mary clasps her arms around Abijah's waist, perches on her toes, and leans in for a kiss.

Elizabeth Jane leaps to her feet and claps her hands.

"Ooh la la!"

"Shhh," Mary says. "Don't you dare say a thing."

"What will you give me?"

"Undying gratitude. Now, skedaddle. Leave us be."

Mary shuts the parlor doors behind the departing children and turns to Abijah. It's only been weeks since they were last together, but he looks older, wiser, windswept, more desirable than before. His ruddy face shows the effects of sea winds and sun.

She pulls him by the hand over to a settee by the window.

"I've missed you so," she says. "Did you miss me?"

"More than I can say."

"I want to know everything." She pulls his folded letter from her bodice. "Especially about this."

"Where shall I—"

"Not here. The children hear everything."

"Tonight then. Come to dinner."

That night, Mary sits alone in her room, her face lit by a single candle. What did she learn at dinner with Abijah's family? They did not meet this woman, Rachel Partridge, only heard about her from Lemuel's cousin. Did the story match what they knew about Ebenezer? The same name— Ebenezer Partridge. The age fits. The business — a merchant — fits. A handsome man from Massachusetts. If the cap fits...

She's heard of men with two wives, two families, two marriages. George once told her about a slave master in North Carolina who had a whole other family in New York, each family a secret to the other. Both families had three children, two girls and one boy, with each pair matching in age and name. Harder to get mixed up that way. George laughed when he told her that. Maybe it was only a joke. But, nevertheless.

But nevertheless, it might be true with Ebenezer. If the cap fits.

So, what can she do? When she was alone with Abijah she asked how she could write to the woman. He said she might write her in care of the cousin's store. That might work.

She has sent letters overseas before. To her father while he was away for a long trip to London. To John when he was away in Barbados. She went to the docks with the letters and paid someone to take them by boat to Halifax. Someone else put them on a ship to the intended destination. It seems a miracle, but they received them.

It must take a long time for a letter to reach Western Massachusetts, but not as long as one sent to London or Barbados. Yes, a letter might get to her, but what should it say?

If I received a letter from an unknown stepdaughter, I would think it a trick or a joke. I would not respond.

A lie might work. A lie based in part on truth. She could write that she is the daughter of Captain Grant, who died a few years ago. She is looking for a man who worked for him, a man by the name of Ebenezer Partridge. Why? What would induce a response? She could pretend to be older, to be the executor of Captain Grant's estate. No, she does not have an official seal for that. Being the daughter will have to be enough. She is a daughter looking for a man named Ebenezer Partridge because he left behind some valuables. Her father, before he died, asked her to return them to him. But he never came back. She learned about her husband from her friend Abijah Scott. She might provide a description of Ebenezer. Then say, if Mrs. Partridge could verify that her husband is the man who worked for her father, she would ensure she received the valuables.

Yes, surely this would trigger a response. But what if she is right that her stepfather is also married to this woman and that Mrs. Partridge gives the letter to him? What would he do? Perhaps he would never return. Good. Perhaps he would confront her when he returns. Also good. Perhaps he would say nothing. But if he knew of the letter, and said nothing, she could tell by his changed demeanor. Something would give it away. All these possibilities are good.

I have nothing to lose.

Chapter Thirty—Four

Submit joins Ebenezer in the study after dinner to discuss business over whiskey and sherry. Ebenezer reports on the orders he has from London for salted cod.

"It's good news that we still have orders," Submit says. "But I'm worried."

"Why is that?"

"Our supply is declining, so we have less to sell."

"Fewer fleets are coming to port with their catches."

"Exactly. I've asked about this with the ship captains at the docks and with our political contacts in Halifax."

"And?"

"The close-in schools are getting fished out, they say. And so, more and more schooners are using purse seines to catch the cod in open sea. They salt and dry the fish on board and head straight to the buyers' ports. They don't need land-based operations like ours. This is the trend of the future."

"I don't disagree, but how do we compete? We don't have the capital to build our own fleet of schooners."

"That's not our only option. We can shift our focus to the lumber trade."

"We already have a good local business in planks and boards. We've done well with that. Where's the growth potential?"

"There's a growing demand in Britain for square lumber and naval masts."

"That's already sourced from the Baltics."

"That has been so, but it's going to change soon. I've been looking into the international developments affecting trade. Napoleon plans on a continental blockade making the Baltic inaccessible to Britain. The war will increase demand and reduce supply, fueling a growth in lumber trade with Canada. By my calculations, annual demand will increase ten times or more in less than ten years."

"How do we take advantage of this? We'll need more labor and equipment to shift from sawn lumber to the shipment of square timber and masts. We don't have the capital for that."

"We can sell the fishery on Helpman's Island. Unload it while its value is still high. Then invest that money in our lumber operations. If we hang on to the fishery our gains will stagnate or even decline. If we increase our investment in our lumber operations we can add to our gains dramatically."

Ebenezer leans back in his chair to ponder his wife's plan. After a short pause, he raises his glass.

"To my wife, the smartest businesswoman in Canada."

"I resent that," she says.

His eyes grow wide.

"Why limit your praise of my business expertise to the category of woman?"

Submit looks out through the east facing windows of the drawing room and admires the view of her favorite scene. The rose garden she planted the summer she married Ebenezer. Ten bushes a year each year since, now sixty, less a few that did not survive the Nova Scotia winters.

The house is quiet. Lily helps the younger children upstairs with a French lesson. Mary is out, as usual, probably at the Scott's house—it doesn't matter where. There is less tension in the air when she is away.

The front door shuts and the floor trembles from the tread of heavy boots. Ebenezer home early.

"Hello, darling," she says. "You're home early."

He leans over her and plants a kiss on her lips.

"I have news," he says.

"I do too. The payments we've been waiting on for our wool finally came through. Smythe delivered the draft himself."

"Here? Why not at the mill?"

"He likes me better than he likes you."

Ebenezer smiles.

"Of course he does. How could he not?"

"And what about you? What's your news? Another broken blade?"

"No. Much better news than that."

"Please tell."

"Abijah came to see me at lunch."

"Is he asking for more money again?"

"No. He asked for permission to marry Mary."

"Goodness. It's about time."

"Knowing your feelings, I thought you'd be pleased."

"More than pleased. What did you say?"

"I said, I was not sure it was my place to grant permission, as I am only her stepfather by marriage. But I assured him he would have my blessing if it was Mary's wish and if you concurred."

"You know I do."

Ebenezer leans forward and takes her hand.

"Abijah is a good match for her, and their fondness for one another has been obvious for some time."

"He does bring a smile to her face on occasion."

"You will be relieved to have her leave?"

"As will you, my dear."

"I admit I would not miss her suspicions and blame."

"Those will remain, I'm afraid."

"They will but they won't be looming over me each day, clouding the air around me, in our own home."

"We agree on that. I love her as a stepmother should love a stepdaughter. Almost as much as a natural mother would. But she makes it so difficult. She is moody and disagreeable with me, and even worse with you, which I especially resent."

"She wants me gone. I know that."

"She wants us both gone. But dear Abijah can save us from that. Tell him soon that we support the marriage without reservation."

"Will you speak with Mary first?"

"That would be a mistake. Whatever I advocate she will resist. It is better that Abijah pushes forward with the union without my intervention. Make him our ally in this."

"I can do that." Ebenezer kisses her hand and guides her up into his arms.

She leans into him.

"It should be a big wedding," she says. "And we should be generous with a wedding gift, something sufficient to bring Abijah to our side."

Mary walks from Grant Hall down to the sawmill. The cotton puffs of cumulus clouds mottle the blue sky. She carries a basket with lunch to share with Abijah—smoked ham, soft cheese, fresh bread, raspberry jam and two bottles of Lily's home brewed ale. Her gait is light, she's almost skipping, in a hurry to see Abijah.

She finds him at the dock loading fresh-cut boards on a barge. He rubs the sawdust from his face and greets her with a kiss. She feels his sweat dampening his coarse shirt. He leads her to a table beside the dock.

"Are we alone?" she asks.

Abijah rifles through the contents of the basket with a smile of approval.

"Yes, Ebenezer has gone to a Mason meeting in Manchester."

"Did you talk?"

"Yes."

"And?"

"Better than expected. They both approve, if you'll have me."

Mary rolls her eyes.

"Anything else?"

He pulls a bottle of ale from the basket and removes the porcelain plug.

"It's a secret."

She swats him on the shoulder. "I hate secrets. What is it?"

"First you have to accept." He squats down on one knee. "Will you marry me?"

She swats him again.

"Yes, of course, you fool." She leans in to plant a kiss on his forehead. "What is it?"

"They intend to give us property and a new house as a wedding gift."

"You're kidding?"

"That's what he said."

"What's the catch?"

"No catch?"

"Where? On the estate?"

"If we want. Or we can have a city lot, near the Church. Our choice."

"City. I don't want to live in their shadow. I wish it were Manchester, or Halifax instead."

"It's best to stay in Guysborough."

"Why?"

"He's offered me a promotion, and a chance to become a partner in the mill. It's a great opportunity for us."

She scrunches the muscles in her face and turns away.

"What is it?" he asks.

"I don't like how this feels."

"How does it feel?"

"Like they'll control us. Like we're puppies leaping up to reach a treat in our master's outstretched hand."

He reaches for her chin and turns her face toward him.

"I don't see the problem. You have always said you felt you did not receive your fair share. Now they offer property and ownership of a good business. Why is this bad? It should be good news."

"I don't know." She throws her hands into the air as if reaching up to God for support. "It shouldn't be theirs to give, and I resent it."

"It does us no good for you to harbor such resentment. Let it go."

She slumps forward with a sigh and accepts his embrace.

"I'm not sure I can," she says in a whisper. He holds her until she leans away.

Part Eight

1810

Chapter Thirty—Five

In the dark of a cold Nova Scotia winter, Submit wakes, alone in bed, under her heavy patchwork quilt. She feels groggy from a vivid dream. She was playing with Henry at the beach. He was two, happy, digging in the sand, toddling to the water's edge. Submit stood close behind to ensure his safety from the waves.

But it's not true. He's dead, less than two years old, buried five days ago in the church cemetery beside his sister Abigail.

She looks around the room. The clothes Ebenezer left on the chair are gone. He has left for work already. He's less affected by grief, or at least hides it better. She admires his strength in this but hates it, too. Why does he not rend his clothes into tatters as the Hebrews do in the Bible? But is it not better to rend your heart than your clothes and do as the Bible says—to return to God for he is gracious and merciful, slow to anger and abounding in love?

If so, why take Henry, why Abigail, why so many that she has known and loved?

She can barely bring herself to move, to think about the day, to do anything other than watch the misty cloud of her breath condensing in the chilly morning air.

But she cannot stay in bed all day. It will be warm in the kitchen, where a fire burns and pots full of the day's provisions simmer.

She finds Lily at work at the kitchen table. Lily offers breakfast but Submit only asks for tea.

Submit takes a chair by the fireplace and sips from the steaming cup. Nearby, Lily prepares her special tinctures. She pulls off the buds and leaves and petals from bundles of dried herbs and flowers she has saved in the cellar—lavender, rose, bergamot. She crushes them with a mortar and pestle, then mixes them with alcohol distilled from wild berries. The smell from the flowers and herbs and alcohol and the cherry wood burning in the fireplace is intoxicating. Submit closes her eyes to absorb the effect.

"Submit, are you well?" Lily asks.

These words bring Submit's attention back to the room.

"Paris," she says. "We must go to Paris."

"What are you talking about?"

"It's time for us to make something of this, of your wonderful concoctions. We've talked about it before. Now is the time to do something. We need to learn about perfume. I need this. You do too. To get over Henry. I'll make plans. We'll leave soon, as soon as the weather permits."

"What about the children?"

"They can stay with Jabez and Margaret. They have a big house. A couple more children won't matter."

She bolts from her chair and spills her cup of tea on the kitchen floor. "I'm sure I have something in the study about the perfume business, some names, some addresses. I will have some breakfast when you have a moment. Something hot. I'll be in the study when it's ready. This will be such fun. We'll both go. Springtime in Paris. Just what the doctor ordered."

The snow on the roof of Mary's new house melts from the lingering warmth of a sunny day and drips on yellow crocuses blooming in the dooryard. Lilacs bud nearby.

Mary is in the kitchen in front of a hot iron stove. The smell of cooked lamb permeates the room. She lifts the lid of a bubbling pot. Her knife slips through a chunk of carrot with only a hint of resistance. She dips a spoon into the pot and tastes the sauce, then adds a pinch of salt. She tastes again. Satisfied, she lifts the pot from the stove. It's heavy and requires the strength of both hands. Her timing is perfect. She sets the pot to the side of the stove to keep warm and hears the front door shut.

"Hello, Mrs. Scott. Your husband has returned."

He leans against the doorway frame. His homespun work clothes are dusty and flecked with sawdust.

"You look dreadful," she says.

He steps closer and pulls her body against him. "And you're quite lovely, too." He strokes her back from the rise of her shoulders to the curve of her rear.

She plants a quick peck on his lips, then pushes him away.

"You stink," she says. "Go change and wash up. Dinner is ready when you are."

While he is upstairs, she sets the table with two pewter chargers, white china bowls, and tall candles.

He descends the stairs sounding like a trotting horse.

"That's better," she says when he enters the dining room. His face is clean, rosy, and damp. He's replaced his dusty clothes with a white shirt and maroon waistcoat. "Now you look lovely too. Light the candles, I'll be right back."

She brings in the stew and serves up bowls for each of them, along with slices of fresh baked bread.

"I didn't expect such a feast," he says and dips a piece of bread in the stew. "Or such a tasty one."

She smiles and nods.

"I learned a lot from Lily growing up. The secret is cinnamon."

After he has finished his second bowl, she brings in a cherry tart and a small pitcher of thick cream.

"I have something I'd like to discuss," she says.

"Of course." He takes a bite of tart and waits for her to continue.

"I've made a decision," she says,

"What is it?"

"Now that spring is here, I've decided to visit the woman in Massachusetts, Rachel Partridge."

He drops his fork onto his plate.

"You can't be serious."

"I am." She folds her arms over her chest.

"Didn't you write to her?"

"I did, years ago."

"Did she write back?"

"She did not. I had no response."

He reaches forward to take her hand.

"Can't you leave it at that?"

"I need to know."

"What good will it do? Look around you. We have a fine house, a good life, great expectations for business and family. Give your attention to that, to us, and not to a silly theory about your stepfather, a man who has been generous to us both."

She pulls her hand away, stands, and snatches the plate with the half-eaten tart away from him.

"I can't let it go. I won't. I'm going to see her with or without you. I'll go alone if I must. Come with me if you wish. Either way, keep your silly insults to yourself."

Chapter Thirty-Six

Mary stands before a mirror in the front hall of their new house and ties the ribbons of a new bonnet below her chin. Abijah enters through the front door.

"Are we ready?" she asks.

"I've loaded the bags. I can't think of anything else."

"Bring that basket. There's bread and cheese and a meat pie for lunch."

He looks over the food, then steps over to a cabinet in the dining room to the side of the front hall and pulls out a bottle.

"Let's not forget the wine," he says.

"Do you need to check in before we go?" she asks.

"No. It's taken care of."

"What did you say?"

"As you said. Before he left for London, I told him we were taking a trip to see my family in Massachusetts."

"A honeymoon."

"Exactly, they couldn't come to the wedding so we're going to see them."

"I said the same to Submit. She said, 'Ah, *un voyage a la façon anglaise,* how wonderful."

He puts the wine bottle in the lunch basket and looks at his pocket watch. "We best be going. The boat leaves for Halifax in less than an hour."

They step outside to a warm spring day. Abijah locks the door behind them. "Do you think she'll come see us off?"

"No. She doesn't care."

"I think Ebenezer would, if he were here."

"And I'm glad he's not."

They board. The horses jerk the carriage forward. Mary looks back at their yellow frame house and sighs. If only she could love it, but she can't. She resents that it was a gift from them.

She turns to Abijah with a new thought. "Do you realize I've never been farther from home than Halifax? I'm quite excited by this. Think of the people we'll meet."

"Indeed. Keep in mind that once we land in Boston we may not be among friends."

"Surely they won't hold our origins against us."

"Surely some may. Tensions are growing between America and the Crown. There's talk of war again."

"We're not involved in that."

"We're still British. And you especially so."

"I've never been to England in my life."

"Still, it would be better if you don't share your family history with strangers."

"Really? I thought I'd tell everyone I meet that my father fought for the British at Bunker Hill. And my brother was an officer in the Cheshire

Regiment of the Foot. Wouldn't that be a good way to make friends?" She glares at him with a satisfied smirk.

"Point taken," he says. "You need no advice from me on your behavior."

She leans over and kisses him on the cheek. "You're a wise man, Mr. Scott."

The carriage turns from the main street of Guysborough to the road leading to the dock. Submit and Lily are waiting. Dressed in colorful silks and large bonnets, they look brilliant in the morning sun. Like gemstones.

"Well, well," Abijah says. "We didn't expect them here, did we?"

"Hmm. They're glad to see us go. She hopes radical Yankees abduct me and I never return."

"Or pirates," Abijah says with a wink.

At their lodgings in Boston, Mary enters the room first and Abijah follows behind with their bags. The room is dark and small, dominated by a high bed with a bare wood frame. She tests the mattress with both hands. It sags to the middle, but the covers are thick.

"It seems clean enough," she says. "I'd prefer more pillows though."

Abijah sets the bags on the floor beside the only window in the room and pulls open the curtains. Sunshine brightens the room.

"There's a good view from here," he says. "Look over there. See the steeple? It's the Old North Church." He turns toward her. "Shall we get out and walk a bit?"

She shakes her head. "You can. I need to rest. The night sail was too rough for me. I couldn't sleep a bit."

"Are you hungry?"

She wraps her arms around his chest and rests her head on his shoulder. "Do you think I could get a cup of warm milk?"

She's disoriented at first when she wakes from her nap. She's alone in a strange room. Where? What time is it? Light filters in around the edges of the drawn curtains. There's a cup beside her on a small bedside table. Now she remembers. This is not her room in Guysborough. She's in Boston now. On a lumpy bed.

Abijah has gone out for the afternoon to visit the waterfront and the merchant offices. He has promised to take her there tomorrow. After that they will leave by coach for Western Massachusetts. They are three days away from Middlefield, the town where Rachel Partridge lives. What will happen when they meet? Will she even meet her?

Of course we will. My plan will work, it must.

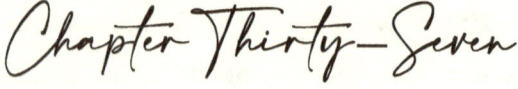

Chapter Thirty-Seven

Three days later they stand in front of a modest frame house in Middlefield, Massachusetts. It's midday. Is Rachel home? How does she live? What does she do with her time? The house is painted white, two stories high, with a black front door flanked by a window on either side and three windows above. The yard is on a small city lot on a side street off the town square.

They knock on the front door, wait, and a woman answers. She wears a drab gray dress with a white apron and white cap.

"Hello ma'am. We're looking for a woman named Rachel Partridge?"

"Who are you?"

"I'm Mary Scott and this is my husband Abijah. I sent a letter about a man named Ebenezer Partridge."

"I don't read, and I don't remember any letter, but I am Rachel Partridge, and my husband' name is Ebenezer. How can I help you?"

"May we come in?"

Rachel invites them into the sitting room. Mary smells hickory smoke from the fireplace. There is a basket of laundry on the floor and folded clothes on a couch.

"I'm sorry for the mess," Rachel says. "It's washing day. Here, please have a seat." She makes room for Mary and Abijah on the couch.

"Would you like tea? I have a hot kettle on the fire in the kitchen. It will only take a moment."

"Thank you, ma'am. That would be most welcome."

Rachel fetches the tea and Mary looks around. There's a rug made from woven rags in the center of the room. Two works of art on the wall— silhouettes of a man and woman, black cutouts on white backgrounds. The man wears a top hat. Could it be her stepfather?

Rachel returns with a teapot, cups and a plate of sweet biscuits. She sets the tray on the small table.

"We'll let it steep a bit. I'm sorry, but I can't offer you any milk. We're out for the moment."

"Thank you, this is more than fine."

There is silence while they wait for the tea to brew. Then Abijah clears his throat and Mary leans forward in her seat.

"Let me explain our visit, Mrs. Partridge," Mary says.

"Please do."

"I wrote some time ago about the situation. You see, there was a man working for my father named Ebenezer Partridge."

"Indeed? Who is your father?"

"Captain William Grant."

"I don't recognize the name. Was he a militia man?"

"No." Mary looks over at Abijah. His look says it all. She should not have said Captain. But she did, so no turning back. She sighs at the weight of the truth.

"No. British regular."

"Where are you from?"

Abijah interrupts. "My people are from near here, militia soldiers in the French and Indian War.

"How interesting. My grandfather was the same. Perhaps they knew each other."

"Perhaps."

Rachel touches the teapot. "This feels ready. Let me pour you a cup."

The others sip their tea and Mary shares her story. Abijah remains silent while she tells her tale. Mary notices him biting his lip as she speaks, relieved that he does not contradict her tale.

"So, you see, Mrs. Partridge, that is why I have written and come to visit. To find the man named Ebenezer Partridge who worked for my father and return his things."

"Something valuable you say?"

"Yes, quite valuable."

"And what is it exactly."

Mary pauses. "I hesitate to say until I'm sure I've found the right man. I trust you can see that."

"I do see. But you've come so far. Did that man who worked for your father say something about me?"

"No, nothing specific as far as I know, only that he was from Massachusetts."

"Did he have a family, any children?"

"Not that I know. My father may have, but he was weak and confused much of the time before he died. I only knew that the man came from Massachusetts. I didn't know how to honor my father's wishes until Abijah came here to visit."

Abijah sets his cup down on the saucer on the side table. "I came here a while back with my family. My uncle runs the general store nearby. I told him about my job with Captain Grant and mentioned that I worked with a man named Partridge. He told me about you. It was a coincidence, actually, that I learned your name."

Mary interrupts. "Abijah told me the story when he got back. When Father died, I wondered if you might know the man. So, I wrote, but I never got an answer. And now that we are married, we decided to visit here to see Abijah's family. And I was still thinking about my father's wish and wondering if it were possible that you might know him." She sets down her teacup and leans forward.

Rachel passes the plate of cookies to Mary, then says, "This is a most remarkable story, Mrs. Scott. And quite a remarkable coincidence of circumstances that led you to me. I would immediately tell you there was no possibility that the man you seek is my husband, if that were so, but in fact—"

"In fact what, Mrs. Partridge?"

"In fact, I don't know."

"So, it is possible?"

"I suppose it is. You see, my husband travels on business often, is often away for a long time, I've not seen him for months."

"What takes him away?"

"He's a merchant. He sells furs mostly, as far as I know."

"Where does he go?"

"I'm not always sure. East of here, of course. Boston, England—"

"Canada?"

"Most probably."

"Guysborough?"

"I've never heard of that place, not until you mentioned it. But I do recall him mentioning Halifax and Port Royal."

"When did you last see him?"

"Last fall, before the cold of winter set in."

"Do you hear from him while he's away?"

"Not much, he's not one to write, and as I said, I don't know how to read. Occasionally I'll hear about him from a traveler who's crossed his path, but nothing during this absence. I worry often when he's away that he will be lost at sea."

Mary leans closer. "So, it does seem possible that your husband is the man I seek. Could you describe him for me?"

"That's his silhouette on the wall, but you can't tell much from that, can you? He's tall, thick black hair, a ruddy complexion. A lovely smile."

"Do you happen to have any papers that he's signed?"

"Yes. There's a desk upstairs in our bedroom. Would you care to come with me to see?"

Rachel leads Mary and Abijah to the bedroom. A wooden, drop-leaf desk stands against the wall. Its open lid reveals pigeonholes stuffed with papers. Rachel removes some and lays them on the desk.

"He may have signed some of these," she says. "You're welcome to take a look."

Mary sees her letter to Rachel among the papers. She lifts it to inspect.

"This is the letter I sent you, Mrs. Partridge. I see it was opened."

"I remember that one. I didn't know what it was and gave it to Ebenezer when we received it. He opened it then."

"What did he say about it?"

"He said it wasn't important. He said he would write back. I didn't think any more about it."

"I did not get a response."

Rachel shrugs. "I don't know if he did, but he said he would."

Mary looks down. It's plausible that he forgot. Or maybe he had secrets to keep. She shuffles through the other papers. One is the envelope addressed to "Ebenezer Partridge, Esq." with a handwritten note on the envelope stating, "Rec'd 10 Jan 09 Ebenezer Partridge."

"Is this his handwriting, Mrs. Partridge?"

Rachel nods.

Mary looks at the letter inside, an order from a man in Salem, Massachusetts, for a shipment of lumber.

"This could be very helpful," Mary says. "We can compare the handwriting with other samples we have in Guysborough."

"You can take it if you wish, if you think it will help."

Mary looks through more of the papers but finds nothing else of note. She squares the pile on the desk. "Is there anything else you can think of to identify your husband?

"Not really. Except that he has a birthmark, right about here." She points to a spot on her lower left belly above the hip. "A red crescent."

Later, when they are standing at the door ready to leave, Mary says, "I can't thank you enough, Mrs. Partridge, for your hospitality. And your assistance."

"I thank you, Mrs. Scott, for your diligence and long journey. If there is something valuable to return, we will be most grateful."

"I'll write when I know more. We'll send a letter to you by way of Abijah's uncle. You can have him read it to you if you'd like."

As they turn to leave, a teenage boy approaches the house. His clothes are dusty and his boots are caked with mud.

"Mrs. Scott, please let me introduce my son, Leo. I'm sorry he's such a mess. He cleans up well."

Leo scowls. "What do you expect? Can't do my work without getting dirty."

"We're pleased to meet you, Leo," Mary says.

Rachel says, "Mrs. Scott and her husband are from Nova Scotia, Leo. They may know your father. How about that?"

Chapter Thirty-Eight

On their journey back to Guysborough, Mary and Abijah stop to visit his uncle. The family hosts a dinner to honor the newlyweds and embrace Mary with affection.

That night the young couple are alone in an extra room above his uncle's store. Mary combs her hair at a wash basin. Abijah asks for her thoughts about the evening.

"It was lovely," she says. "Everyone was so kind."

"I'm glad. I wondered. You seemed miles away."

"I'm tired from travel."

He stands behind her and massages her shoulder muscles. "It's more than that. Isn't it?"

She stands and wraps her arms around his waist. "I learned much from Mrs. Partridge. I learned facts that will prove Ebenezer's double life."

Abijah pulls away.

"I wish we had learned more," he says. "I wish we had learned that your theory was impossible. I wish her husband had answered the door so you would see for yourself that he was a different man."

"But we didn't learn that, did we? We learned that they could be the same man. We learned that her husband fits the description. We learned that he is a merchant. That he travels to Canada. That he is gone for months on end."

She grabs him by the arm and pulls him closer.

"Her husband could have been a farmer. A shopkeeper. Home every night for supper. Beside her every night in bed. But he is not. He could have been a man with blond hair, or red, or bald, but he is not. A man with bad teeth, for God's sake."

Abijah opens his mouth to speak, but she covers it with her palm.

"But instead," she says. "But instead, we learned this—based on these facts, it is more likely than not that he is the same man. That is what we know."

Her voice rises and the words come too fast for Abijah to respond. When she finally releases him, he is without words.

She takes the envelope from her handbag. "Here, tell me that this is not Ebenezer's signature. You work with him. You should know his signature well."

"I can't. It could be. I can't tell."

"And the birthmark. Have you seen him disrobed? Do you know?"

"I have not. I don't know."

"Neither do I. But Submit will know. If confronted with these facts, if she sees the signature, if she is told about the birthmark, she will know. Whether she admits it or not, she will know the truth."

"And what will be gained? Really, what?"

"Much. She will doubt him. Hate him. Reject him. Know that he's a liar. And if he is a liar about this, then she will wonder, is he a liar about my father's death?"

He sits on the edge of the bed, head bowed, face covered by the palms of his hands.

"Mary, Mary, Mary." He shakes his head, then looks up into her eyes. "Don't you see. Nothing good can come of this. You can't change the past. You can only destroy the future. Our future. They have been good to us. Why destroy that?"

"Why? You ask, why? What would you have me do? Remain silent? Do nothing? What would you do if your father died, and you knew that your stepfather had killed him? What would you do then?"

Chapter Twenty-Nine

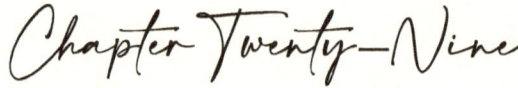

Mary and Abijah travel in a horse-drawn wagon driven by their uncle's neighbor, Silas Hatfield, from Middlefield to Deerfield. It's a long slow ride. Mary and Abijah stay overnight at Barnard Tavern in Deerfield. Hatfield stays too, waiting for morning to return to Middlefield. Once settled they meet for dinner—fresh bread and a dark brown stew filled with carrots and onions and chunks of venison. A few pints of ale lubricate Hatfield's tongue.

"It's a good thing, Miss, if you don't mind my saying so, that you're not traveling alone."

"Why is that Mr. Hatfield?"

"You just never know."

"Never know what?"

"Indians. Pirates maybe. You never know what you'll run into once you get on the water."

Abijah leans forward, arms crossed on the table. "Surely, sir, there's no risk of danger on this route."

"Well, like I say, you never know."

He downs the rest of his ale and signals for another mug.

"Why just the other day, I was in town and heard an old timer, a fellow named Josiah Smith, tell a story to a group of schoolboys over at the General Store. He said when he was young, he worked as a cabin boy on the crew of a merchant ship sailing up and down the Connecticut coast. He said, one time he was beached on an island off the coast during a storm. As soon as the weather cleared, a boat load of pirates attacked."

He lets that sink in and grins.

"One of the boys listening said, 'What did you do?' Josiah said, 'We had to fight for our lives, we did.' The boy asked, 'Did you fight too, or did you hide?' Josiah said, 'I was in it with the best of them' The boy asks, 'Did you have guns to scare them off?' Josiah said, 'None that worked, due to the storm. We fought them off with swords and boards and our bare fists. I'm lucky to be alive.'"

Hatfield snorts to punctuate the point.

"Then the boy asked, 'Did you get hurt?' And Josiah leaned forward, and said, 'Did I? See that?' He pointed to a scar on his left cheek, and said, 'Slashed with a pirate's cutlass, I was. Nearly bled to death. If I hadn't been unconscious on the ground, the pirate crew would have hauled me away. That's how they recruit new pirates, don't you know. By kidnapping young boys.'"

Hatfield glares bug-eyed at Mary, as if to say, what do you make of that Missy?

"At this point the boys are wide eyed, their mouths agape. So, I stepped up, and I said, 'Josiah, that's enough of your tall tales. I know full well you got that scar falling out of an apple tree.'"

Hatfield struggles to get through the punch line before he convulses in a fit of laughter.

Abijah leans back and smiles.

Mary says, "Mr. Hatfield, I do believe you've told that story a time or two."

Still chuckling, he says, "Yes, Miss. I confess I have."

In the morning, Hatfield helps Mary and Abijah take their bags to the boat landing. Before heading back to Middlefield, he says, "watch out for them thar pirates, matey." This triggers another bout of convulsive laughter ending with a fit of coughing and gasping for air as he pulls away with the wagon.

Mary and Abijah travel down the Connecticut River by shallop, passing Northampton, Springfield, and Agawam, until they reach Enfield Falls, where they transfer the passengers and cargo to a larger ship.

They spend a night in East Haddam, Connecticut. The next morning, they attend a church service. Reverend Calvin Brainerd delivers a sermon. He preaches about the controversy over the true path reach God. Whether it's through grace or good deeds. According to him, neither is the right way. Instead, believing in Jesus Christ is the one true path. From this belief, all divine blessings come, including feeling God's grace and motivation to do good.

Their final stop on the river before entering Long Island Sound is Old Saybrook. They change boats there and sail out of the harbor past the lighthouse at Lynda Point. The Sound is calm when they leave the River for open waters, but there is a wall of black clouds behind them to the

West. One of the crew warns them strong winds are approaching and should blow them out past the islands to Cape Cod faster than expected. "Be ready for rough seas," he says.

The storm chases behind them as they rush ahead with the ship's large sails full of wind. The bow breaks through mounting waves sending clouds of mist into the air. Mary and Abijah leave the wet deck for their small room below deck. They have one small porthole window looking onto the wake of the ship. They struggle to maintain balance as the ship rises and falls with the waves. Mary feels sick and lies down on the narrow bottom bunk in the cabin.

"Come with me," Abijah says. "We should get you some fresh air, even if we get soaked."

She sits up, sets his feet on the floor, buckles over clutching her belly, and vomits into a bucket beside the bed. She sinks to the floor, keeping the bucket nearby.

Abijah offers water, but she refuses.

This continues for hours, then the swells begin to calm. The violent roll of the ship has weakened into a gentle rock. Sunlight comes into the cabin through the porthole.

A crew member comes by their cabin.

"The worst is over," he says. "Smooth sailing now. We've rounded the Cape, and the storm has moved south. You're welcome on deck if you wish."

Mary relaxes as the waves relax, takes some water, and keeps it down.

Abijah asks, "How are you doing? Better?"

She nods. "I'd rather fight pirates and Indians, though."

Mary and Abijah arrive in Boston and disembark with their luggage. It's mid-morning, clear and bright, with no sign of last night's storm.

Chapter Forty

They ride by wagon to the Inn where they stayed when they first arrived in Boston. Mary is still not feeling well and vomits after eating some soup and bread. Abijah wants to find a doctor, but she claims she'll be fine. The only thing she needs is rest.

By early afternoon, still hours from sunset, she feels better, wants to get out, breathe fresh air. She has an address for Ebenezer's business and crude directions provided by the Tavern owner.

They take a winding path to the harbor. The waterfront is busy with arriving and departing ships, passengers embarking and disembarking. Horses pull wagons loaded with luggage and goods. Men lift pallets of supplies up to ships with the help of block and tackle. Dirty-faced young boys in tattered clothes sell apples and small loaves of bread to well-dressed ladies and gentlemen boarding ships.

But when they arrive at the address, the business office Mary expects to find is not there. Instead, it's an empty office available to rent. A door next to the empty office leads upstairs to where the landlord sits, a bearded and bald man, behind a desk piled high with papers.

"I'm pretty new here," he says. "That office has been empty since I started this job. It was your father, you say?"

"Stepfather," Mary says. "One of them was. He had partners in the business."

"I must have something here about them." He rifles through a ledger on this desk. "Here it is. The record of their account. They haven't been here for over a year but left paid in full. No problem there. I thought I might have something here to show where they went, but there's nothing."

"Can you remember anything?"

"Like I say, I wasn't here at the time, and we manage lots of offices along the wharf. I don't have much call to track moves of tenants who've paid up."

"Can you think of anyone else I could ask?"

"The owner of the building might know something, but he lives up in Gloucester. I'd say you best check at the Customs House."

He gives them directions on a slip of paper.

"It's only a short walk," he says.

Once there, they meet Thomas Melville, the Naval Officer of the Port, a man in his sixties with a long, thin face and long white hair that sweeps over his balding head.

"Partridge? Yes, I know a business by that name. I'd be glad for the chance to stretch my legs and show you the way."

They soon arrive at a well-tended brick building several streets away. There is a tailor shop on the ground floor. Mr. Melville points up to the second floor.

Mary looks up. The second-floor window bears the trade name in gold letters: "Partridge, Tuthill & Welles."

Mr. Melville asks, "May I do anything else to assist?"

"No, thank you. You're most kind indeed, but we can go on from here."

"Very well." He doffs his hat and offers his hand. "Please call on me if I can be of further service."

The stairs to the left of the tailor shop lead up to the merchants' offices. A clerk sitting at a desk in the front anteroom of the business offices greets them.

"May I help you?"

"Yes, I hope so," Mary says. "I am looking for Ebenezer Partridge. Do you know him?"

"Of course, he is one the partners."

"Is he here?"

"No, he left for Maine a while ago and then—" The man pauses, lost for words. "You should speak with one of the partners."

He offers them chairs and then takes leave to the back offices. Mary glances around as she waits. Paintings of sailing ships hang on a wall. Stacks of ledgers lean against another behind the desk.

The clerk returns with a gentleman.

"Good morning. I'm John Tuthill, one of the owners. How may I help you?"

Mary steps forward. "I'm looking for Ebenezer Partridge."

"One of my partners. May I ask what this regards?"

"I am Mrs. Scott. This is my husband Abijah Scott. My stepfather is Ebenezer Partridge. We're visiting Boston from Nova Scotia, and I was hoping we could see him while we're in town."

"I see. May ask where your stepfather lives?"

"Guysborough, Nova Scotia, where we live."

Mr. Tuthill's eyes widen at this news. He looks at the clerk, who shrugs, then gathers his composure.

"It would be best if we could discuss this in my office."

She hesitates. "I only need to know how to find him. I don't mean to cause you any trouble."

"It's complicated," he says. "Please come with me and we'll sort things out."

Tuthill's office overlooks the street and has a view of masts in the harbor at the end of the street. She accepts a chair and Tuthill sits at his desk.

"I must say, Mrs. Scott. I'm rather confused."

"As am I."

"Well, madam, our Ebenezer Partridge travels for the firm. Sometimes he stops in Halifax. But he lives in Massachusetts."

"Do you know his family?"

"Yes, he has family in Middlefield. His wife's name is Rachel, although we've never met. I've never heard of any stepchildren."

"Indeed." She glances at Abijah, then turns back to Mr. Tuthill. "What does he look like?"

"Tall, dark hair."

"Does he have a birthmark on his hip?"

"Goodness. I have no idea about that."

"When did you last see him?"

"A few months ago, I'd say. It's common for him to be away for quite a long time."

"Do you hear from him often?"

"He writes about business from time to time. I can show you some of his letters if you'd like to check the handwriting."

He goes to a cabinet and removes a stack of papers.

"Here's the most recent letter we have." He pulls out one from the top of the stack. "It arrived several months ago, but we've had nothing since. In any event, it appears to me that he is not the man you seek. Is there anything else I can do for you?"

When they get outside, Mary hauls Abijah around the corner of the building and pulls him close.

"That proves it," she says.

"Proves what?"

The words fly from her. "They are the same man, my stepfather and Rachel's husband. Don't you see? They have the same office!"

Abijah shakes his head.

She shakes him by his lapels. "The address we have for our Ebenezer is the office of Rachel's husband. You must see that? The facts fit. Mr. Tuthill told us the man he knows comes from Middlefield. And the letter he showed us, the handwriting is the same as his." She pulls the letter Rachel gave her out of her purse. "Here. Tell me it's not the same."

Abijah cups Mary's face in his hands.

"Yes, darling," he says. "The handwriting was the same. They were from the same man. But it was not the same office."

She pushes away. "But it was," she says. "Of course it was. We went straight there following directions to my stepfather's office."

"Come with me," he says. "Let's get back to our room. You need rest."

That evening Abijah has dinner brought to the room. But Mary eats little, then vomits into the chamber pot. Abijah sits on the bed beside her, relieved that she sleeps through the night. A day later she can eat again and says she is ready to travel, so Abijah reserves passage on the next ship to Nova Scotia.

When they finally reach home in Guysborough, Mary sends word of their return to Grant Hall. Lily soon arrives at the house while they are unpacking from the trip.

"Welcome back," Lily says. She makes a fine impression dressed in a blue and black silk dress with a matching handbag, shoes and bonnet.

Mary invites her into the sitting room.

"How was your journey?" Lily takes a seat on the sofa.

"Long. Dreadful. I'm exhausted." Mary sits opposite her. "How are things here?"

"Much changed. I suppose you traveled through Boston?"

"Yes, we boarded our ship to Halifax there."

"We didn't know how to reach you to let you know that your mother was there too."

Mary chaffs at this—Submit is not her mother—but lets it pass. She waits for Lily to continue.

"She was close to giving birth and doing well. But given the sad fate of their first two children, Ebenezer thought it best for her to give birth in

Boston. He knows a well-known doctor there, Dr. Comfort Starr. He invited them to stay with him until Submit and the new baby were fit to travel. They returned last week with a wonderful baby boy. They've named him Joseph Arlington.

"Goodness! I wish I had known."

"Of course. You could have met up in Boston to help. But never mind. You can be a help here if you're willing. We could use another set of hands, and eyes."

"Of course. I'll be glad to help, once I get some rest."

"Whenever you're ready. In the meantime, I imagine you could use some help as well. You must have clothes in need of washing."

"Loads and loads. I only just dumped the dirty things on the bedroom floor."

"Fine. Show me the way. We'll bundle it up in a sheet and send it up to the house. We can have everything clean and fresh for you in no time."

A few hours later, with Abijah away at the Mill, Mary submits to her exhaustion and the onset of a migraine. She wants to write a letter to Rachel, so she finds pen and paper and sits at the desk in her sitting room. But the aura of the migraine distorts her vision. She settles down on the couch to rest with her eyes closed. But she cannot put these thoughts aside.

She dozes then wakes in a fever unsure where she is. Then she remembers. She has returned from church. Why was she there? She's confused. It was a funeral. For Ebenezer. She remembers now. He caught a fever at sea and died upon return.

Her mind spins and will not release her until she gets word to Mrs. Partridge. Abijah will not approve, of course. He will say, now at long last, the man is dead, can you not give up your quest? She cannot. The man may be dead but that is not the end. Submit must know the truth and suffer as she has suffered from the murder of her father. Submit will refuse to listen. of course. She will reject the evidence Mary has brought back from Massachusetts. But what if Submit were confronted with the facts by Rachel Partridge? That might change everything.

Mary thinks this through. Rachel is Ebenezer's first wife based on the age of Leo. That means that Submit's marriage to Ebenezer is invalid. And that would mean that the estate of Ebenezer, all the business ownership that was transferred to him when he married Submit would go to Rachel, not Submit.

She will do this—seek revenge for her father's death—even if she loses as a result. But might she and Abijah benefit from this? Rachel would own Ebenezer's interest in the Grant family businesses. Rachel would own the mill. And she would need help. Abijah could take over on her behalf.

And Submit? She would finally have to face the fact that Ebenezer was a bigamist, dishonest in love, dishonest in life, a man who would kill another for gain then lie about it without remorse.

Mary has much to gain by pursuing this. But she cannot make it happen on her own. She must convince Rachel to stake a claim. She is not sure she can do that. But she can try.

Her headache has grown worse, and she feels a fever coming back. Still, she rises from the couch, picks up the pen to take the first step.

Dear Mrs. Partridge,

I have important news to share with you about Mr. Ebenezer Partridge. The man by that name who has lived among us in Guysborough passed away from a brief illness and was buried today. If your husband is with you now this coincidence will be of no particular interest to you. However, if your husband has not returned from his travels since our visit with you, I believe we can conclude with certainty that they are the same man. In that event, I urge you to travel to Guysborough at your earliest convenience to determine the truth and make your claim against his estate.

Sincerely,

Mary Scott

Exhausted by the effort the letter took to write, she reclines the couch. Her mind finds comfort in her scheme and in the thought of what comes next until her fever takes over.

Chapter Forty-Two

M ary stirs in her bed and cries out.

"They are the same man. You are—were—both married to the same man. Look at Leo, look at his face, don't you see, his eyes, his mouth, he's Ebenezer's son, he's your husband's son. Can't you see that?"

Abijah rushes into the room.

Her cries continue. "He's your husband's son. He's your husband's son."

Abijah kneels beside her.

"Mary. Mary. I'm here. Everything will be fine."

He places his hand on her forehead.

"Your fever is gone, Mary.

She opens her eyes.

"Where am I? How did I get here?"

"You're home. In our bedroom. You've been here for days."

"I was with Rachel Partridge. And Submit. In Submit's parlor."

"No."

"But I was."

"No, you've been here. I found you in the living room."

"But I wrote her a letter. And she came. She came to claim her husband."

"There's no letter and she's not here."

"I wrote a letter. To Rachel."

"I found pen and paper on the table, but no letter."

"Nothing?"

He shook his head. "You've been ill. You had a bad fever. What you're thinking now, it must have been a dream, you must have been imagining it."

"How long?"

"Two days, going on three. Submit came both days, while I was at work. She says she sat by your bed, held your hand, tried to feed you broth."

"Did I say anything?"

"Just now, yes. You we're saying— 'He's your husband's son.' You said it over and over."

"Did I say anything to Submit?"

"I don't know, I was at work. She didn't say anything to me about it if you did."

Chapter Forty-Three

Submit arrives early the next morning at the Scott house carrying a long-handled wicker basket. She enters without knocking, knowing Abijah is at work at the mill. Mary sits at the table in front of a pot of tea.

Good, it is better this way. If she is well enough to get up from her sick bed, she is well enough for this encounter.

"Ah," she says, with the energy of a cheerful cardinal, "the patient has returned. So good to see."

"I didn't know I was away," Mary says. "But I am here, as you can see."

"And it is good to see that you are better. We've been so worried the past few days."

"I'm sure you have been."

"Of course I have. You must know I've been here every day at your side."

"Abijah has told me so."

"He needed help. And I've seen more than my share of illness and death, as you know."

"You've become an expert. I marvel that you could find the will to care for me."

Submit does not rise to the bait. The attitude of this girl is impossible, after all they have done for her. Yet it does not serve her purpose to react, not yet.

She sets the basket on the table before Mary. "I've brought you a few things to help you regain your strength. Fresh bread, raspberry preserves, and butter."

Mary lifts the cloth that drapes over the edge of the basket. "I've had my breakfast, but this will be welcome later, I'm sure."

Submit purses her lips and takes a seat at the table.

"I do this out of love. Love for you, Abijah, all your siblings."

"You've played your role," Mary says, "and reaped your—"

Submit waves her hand to cut her off.

"I'll concede at first it was out of duty. I was my father's dutiful daughter. But I have grown to love you all." She pauses and smiles. "Even you, as hard as that may be for you to believe. The same is true for Ebenezer, he loved your father and has loved all of you as I have."

Submit pulls the basket close to her and breaks off a piece of bread.

"It is still warm," she says, "Care to try some?"

Mary shakes her head, leans back in her chair, arms folded across her chest.

"We have been generous to you," Submit says. "You must agree to that. Raised you in comfort, provided you with this house, given Abijah a fine job and a sound future, and yet—"

"You only share a piece of what you stole from my family, nothing more."

"Hush!" Submit leans forward to cut her off.

"Your father and mine made a fair bargain for my services. I received what your father intended, nothing more. And we—Ebenezer and I—took that legacy, of what, a sawmill and a fishery, and made it so much more, much more than you or your soldier brother could have attained."

"What would you and Abijah have done on your own? Made a living selling boards from a backwater dock? We built your father's holdings into textiles, mining, shipping. And we've given you and Abijah a chance to be part of that."

Mary remains speechless, jaw clenched. Submit continues.

"But not only that. We have offered you our love, although you have made that so hard to do, with your delusions of mistreatment and your quest for revenge where none is due."

"I have no delusions," Mary says.

"Oh, no? And what of this?" Submit pulls a sheet of folded paper from the sleeve of her dress. She pushes it across the table to Mary. "It's written in your hand, is it not? You left it on the table when you fell ill. I found it there when I came to care for you. Go ahead, read it. You can't have forgotten so soon."

Submit watches Mary unfold the letter.

"This delusion of yours—that we have stolen your family estate, that we have killed your father, that Ebenezer has a secret family—it is all a sick fantasy of your making, nothing more, and it has gone too far. It is bad enough that you impose your delusion on me, but with that letter you would impose it on innocent strangers. You're going beyond sullen hatred to wicked cruelty."

She leans toward Mary and says in a forced whisper, "And it must stop. Now."

Mary says nothing and Submit snatches back the letter.

"Thank God, you never sent this."

Submit stands to take her leave. When she reaches the door, she turns back to Mary. "If you'd like proof of your grandest delusion, please join us for dinner on Saturday. Ebenezer will be back from Halifax. You will find him quite alive."

Abijah returns that night at sundown from the mill. Mary is up, pacing around the front parlor, mumbling.

"Hello darling. Are you well enough to be up and about? You should still be resting?"

"That beastly witch came here today."

"Who?"

"She says I'm deluded."

"About what?"

"I can't believe you let her sit at my bedside while I was sick."

"She was kind to do it."

"Kind?" She turns to glare at him. "She did it only in hopes of watching me suffer. Or die."

"Let me make you something. Some tea. While you sit and relax. Please."

"No tea. I don't want anything." She flails her arms in the air as she speaks.

"Please sit and tell me what this is all about."

He takes her arm and leads her to the sofa. She sits, takes a deep breath, lets her body slump. He strokes her shoulder.

"Tell me, darling, what has stirred you so?"

"I'm not sure I dare. You will side with her."

"Only if you both are on the same side."

"But we are not." She stands and faces him. "She says I am deluded because I believe Ebenezer may have—may have had—a secret life. We know he did, he had many secrets, we are just not sure what they were. But that doesn't matter. That misses the point."

"What point?"

"The fact that Submit and Ebenezer conspired to steal my father's legacy from his true family. The fact that they killed him."

"You don't know that darling. You can't know that."

"I know for certain that they ended up with all that my father had made. You can't deny that."

"I can deny that they stole it."

"But they have it, and that is more than enough of a motive for all the rest. She meets a young, handsome man. My father conveniently dies. And then she remarries in less than four months. Who does that?"

Abijah is silent. He slumps forward, closes his eyes, and shakes his head.

"A black widow does that," she says. "An evil spider who kills her mate, then soon finds another."

He looks up at her with eyes wide in disbelief.

"I'll tell you this," she says. "I may not be able to prove it, but I know it is so. And even if I am the only one shouting against the wind, I will never forget. Or forgive. As long as I live, I will never forgive."

"All things heal with time."

"This will never heal."

A week later, Mary is reading the front parlor when Abijah returns from work to share his midday dinner with her.

"I have news for you," he says. "You'll say it doesn't matter, that it doesn't change your mind. But it is something you should know and consider. I received news today from my uncle in Massachusetts."

He takes a letter from his jacket and hands it to her.

"He says that Mr. Ebenezer Partridge of Middlefield returned to his wife and family shortly after our visit. Apparently, they have since relocated to Pike County in Western New York."

She scowls and opens the short letter, only a few lines of neat handwriting, then looks up.

"So what?" She tosses it back at him. "What if my theory about his marriage to Rachel is a mistake, a silly fantasy, a feverish delusion. This changes nothing. Nothing at all regarding the essential point. This is not over, not at all."

Chapter Forty-Four

January 11, 1810

Dearest Submit,

I am so happy to have received news from you, and such wonderful news! I gladly accept your proposal. I have been away too long and am ready to return. It will be a pleasure to help you with my new nephew! I'll let you decide if I should teach Joseph French or German. I will be there as soon as sail and wind can carry me.

His favorite auntie,

Huldah

Huldah sets a lit candle on the nightstand in her bedroom at Grant Hall, pulls back the quilt, and eases into the soft bed with a deep sigh. She opens her book to the place saved by a leather bookmark and rereads the last paragraph.

There is a light rap on the door. Submit peers into the room.

"May I come in?"

"Of course." Huldah props herself up against the pillows.

"How was your day?" Submit asks, stepping over to the left side of the bed.

"Good," Huldah says. "Busy, tiring."

"The children can be exhausting." She brushes a lock of Huldah's hair off her forehead.

"May I sit?"

Huldah pats the bed beside her.

"I've been meaning to tell you," Submit says. "Looking for a time to tell you."

Huldah wrinkles her brow. "What is it?"

"I've heard from our cousin."

Huldah closes her book and says nothing.

"She wrote about a few things you had not mentioned."

"What might that be?"

"Your time in the convent. Your child."

"She did?"

"Is that true, that you were with child, that you found shelter in a convent?"

"It was not my plan."

"But it is the truth?"

"I was in love with him. Or at least I thought so. You must understand that."

Submit reaches out and clasps Huldah's hands in hers.

"I understand love, and I understand your loss."

"It's not the same. That is why I kept my secret. You had a loving husband by your side, to hold your hand, to comfort you."

"And you did not. I know it's not the same."

"It's not the same at all. For me it was sinful."

"I don't believe that. Did you love him?"

"Yes, at the time, very much."

"Then it was not a sin." Submit looks down and smooths the blankets beside her. "Our cousin says your child was adopted. We can believe she is happy, healthy, living with a family that loves her."

"But our cousin does not know all."

Submit looks into Huldah's eyes. "What do you mean?"

"She does not know about the first. There was another, from my first trip."

"A different man?"

"No, the same. There was only one man, the one I love — loved. That child—the first child—died."

"Oh, my dear!" She clasps her hands on Huldah's cheeks and bows her head low so that their foreheads touch. Both start to cry.

"Was it a boy?" Submit asks.

"Too early to tell."

"Oh Lord, how sad for you." They embrace each other and say nothing for several moments. The candle sputters beside them.

Finally, Huldah pulls away and wipes her eyes.

"I can pack in the morning and leave tomorrow. I'm sure you will not want me here now."

"Don't be silly. This binds us as sisters, even closer than we were before. We have both lost children who blessed our wombs. That is a bond we shall never break. I want you here, I need you here. This is where you belong now, so you can heal. You will stay here as long as you wish. Together we can both heal."

Huldah pulls her sister close and kisses her forehead.

"Bless you," she says. "It is a relief that I can finally share this with you."

In the Spring, the ladies of Grant Hall relax in the back parlor, each beside the flickering light of a taper. Most of the children went to bed without fuss. Joseph fought sleep but he too is quiet now. Submit reads about the growing tensions between Britain and America in the newspaper. Lily is reading *Candide* in French. Huldah leafs through a well-worn book with loose pages, many dog-eared.

Submit watches her struggle to keep the book in order. "Your Mrs. Wollstonecraft may need a replacement," she says.

Huldah smiles. "It can't bear to part with it. It holds my margin notes."

"You are not teaching this to your pupils, are you?"

"I don't have them read it, of course. I'd surely be tarred and feathered."

"But—?"

"But I do try to follow her guidance about educating women."

"Such as?"

"As a start, show them that an educated woman is the equal of a man."

"And what do the boys think of that?"

"They snigger and smirk, but they too learn that an enlightened, educated man knows this is true."

"A good lesson to learn."

"It makes me glad to be living without a man," Huldah says. "I suppose I should have been a nun if I were Catholic."

Submit smiles. "I remember our last walk on the beach before I married. Do you remember what you said?"

Huldah shakes her head.

"You said you were sure you would marry before you were twenty."

"I'm not much at predictions, am I?"

"You are too much of a romantic for that. Unlike me. I pursued the path of duty, of submission to our father's will. You chased love."

"Your life has turned out the better for it."

"Yours is not over. You can't yet say which is better."

Lily nods. "We are what we are. We cannot change the past, only learn from it, accept what is, and endeavor to make the future better."

"Well said, my dear. We have many opportunities before us and much to look forward to."

The wail of a child interrupts their conversation. The women listen a moment, but the cries continue. Submit rises from her chair.

"Duty calls. I'll see if I can lull him back to sleep."

Huldah watches her leave the room, then says, "We all struggle with our duties, don't we Lily? Duty to our parents, our family, our children."

Lily sets her book to the side. "And once you come to terms with that, the struggle continues, as you deal with the challenge of freedom and independence, of being unfettered. Of being alive. The struggle is a vindication of your rights as a person. How you choose to act in the face of it is what matters."

"It all seems to me that my fate is controlled by destiny, or the hand of God, or something beyond my control. I don't see that I have a choice."

Lily leans forward to clasp her hand. "There's only one way to find out."

Later that night, Huldah sits alone in her room at her desk and mulls over Lily's thoughts on choice. She hears echoes in her mind of her friends reading by Lac Leman in Geneva. She finds the book on the shelf in her room. *The Discourses of Epictetus.* The page is still marked. Her memory was correct. The passage reads:

"Consider who you are. Above all, a human being, carrying no greater power than your own reasoned choice, which oversees all other things, and is free from any other master."

She closes the book and slips it back in its place on the shelf.

She retakes her seat at the desk. Beside her is a copy of the *Halifax Gazette*, open to an advertisement she saw earlier in the day for a position as tutor at the University of King's College in Windsor. Interested parties may apply by post to the Right Reverend John Inglis D.D., Bishop of Nova Scotia. Huldah runs her finger across the words. Would they hire a woman? Would they take me? Hard to say, but they won't unless I apply.

Above all . . . You have the power of choice . . . free from any other master.

She can choose to do nothing, or she can take up her pen and a sheet of paper from the box Submit gave her more than a decade ago. She moves the candle closer and lifts the pen.

Chapter Forty—Five

Submit walks back from a meeting at church and sees a crowd clustered outside the Courthouse. She steps up behind a woman carrying a wooden wash basin on her hip. The crowd blocks Submit's view of an official notice nailed beside the courthouse door.

"What is it?" she asks.

The wash woman steps aside so Submit can read. The large print at the top of the page says, "America Declares War on Crown."

The blacksmith call out, "Good news, I say. They beat them once; they can do it again."

The tavern owner shouts him down. "You're a fool, McGill. The King rules the sea. The Yanks will never get close."

"There are plenty places to attack without hitting the high seas."

Another man yells out. "I say you ought to leave town if you feel that way. Take the next packet to Boston before you're boiled in tar."

The blacksmith barks back. "This will all be over before I have time to pack my bags."

"It might be over fast, but not the way you like it. The Crown focuses on its battle with Napoleon in Europe. It won't or can't bother with us. There will be a peace soon, I tell you, and we'll end up part of America, whether any of you like it or not."

Submit ignores the shouting and steps close to read the handbill. President Madison and Congress declared war on Britain on June 18, 1812. The Conservative government in Britain calls for an embargo on American goods. Canadian Loyalists will prosper from a privileged position to supply fish, livestock, lumber and grain to Britain under the protection of the King's navy. Lord Dorchester calls on all Canadians to support the Crown in preserving Britain's position in Canada:

"The only firm hold that Great Britain has upon the remains of the American Dominions is certainly by means of the Loyalists."

Submit smiles and turns away from the arguing men choosing sides. She cares little about their debate. A long. lingering battle will free them from competition with the Americans. Their business with Britain will boom.

Months later, Ebenezer returns early from the mill. He finds Submit in the study.

"It's all here," he says, pulling the Halifax Gazette out of his carrier bag.

"America's attacks on Canada have all failed. Hull falls to Brock at Detroit. They say it's likely he'll be court-martialed for cowardice and neglect of duty."

He points to paper.

Rensselaer's assault at the Niagara River fails. Over nine hundred American troops captured and three hundred killed. Dearborn's plan to capture Montreal ends on the shores of Lake Champlain. His troops retreat without even entering Canada. The whole thing on the American side is a fiasco, nothing but 'disaster, defeat, disgrace, and ruin and death.'"

Submit scans the paper while Ebenezer paces the room, full of praise for the British and Canadian troops.

"Any more of this, and the War will be over before winter."

Submit peers at him over the top of her reading glasses. "For the troops' sake, I hope so. But it won't be good for us."

"Why? Our business is booming."

"Exactly, because of the War. Peace with America could be our ruin."

"There's not much we can do."

"Not to affect or deflect the peace, true. But we can plan for the likely decline in business."

"Something could come of Burr's efforts in Europe to free Mexico from Spain, opening that market up to us."

"Perhaps. But I'm not betting on that horse."

Submit drops by the mill carrying a basket of lunch for Ebenezer. He's seated at his desk busy with invoices. She sets the latest edition of the *Gazette* in front of him.

"More bad news from the West." she says. "So much for the War being over. The Americans have finally left York, leaving it in ruins after burning and looting the town. Women and children and unarmed civilians killed. Is there no honor in War anymore?"

Ebenezer lifts the checkered cloth covering his lunch.

"I'm not surprised," he says. "The American's were humiliated at Detroit and Niagara and Montreal. They wanted revenge."

"I am surprised. You should be too. We both were Americans before we were Canadians. We both loved an honorable British soldier, me as a wife, you as a friend. We know he would not have treated innocents in such a manner. There was a time when I would have been happy if Canada surrendered to the Americans and became part of the United States. But this treatment of York leaves a bad taste. I can see no union now, and do not wish it."

Ebenezer scans the front-page news.

"According to this, the occupation lasted two weeks. They burned the Legislative Assembly and the Government House – the home of the Lieutenant Governor, for God's sakes! Smashed the presses at the Official Printing Office. Looted empty houses. Destroyed most of the structures in the fort. Nothing good will come of it, I wager."

April 1814. Ebenezer retires to the parlor after a dinner of roast lamb and new potatoes. Submit hands him the daily news from Halifax, then turns to the view of the sunset through the parlor window.

"I would say that changes everything."

Ebenezer pours himself a glass of whiskey from the sideboard.

"I'm not so sure. The Canadian militia has been holding its own since York."

"But only that," she says. "We've been at a standstill."

Ebenezer hands back the newspaper and points to final paragraphs.

"According to this, it was very different than York. Ross led the occupation. A proper officer and gentleman. He entered Washington with a flag of truce and forty-five hundred men. Yet the foolish Americans fired on them. So, the British burned public buildings, of course. But Ross insisted that private buildings were not disturbed. And they only stayed four days."

Submit points to the last line of the article.

"The paper quotes Bishop Strachan in Toronto. The attack on Washington was a small retaliation after redress had been refused for burnings and depredations in York, not only of public but private property, committed by them in Canada. That sounds about right to me."

Ebenezer takes a gulp of whiskey

"I'd say the end is close. With Napoleon defeated and exiled in Alba, Britain can commit more ships and troops to North America, free to show its strength and exact retribution for York and all the rest."

Submit a seat facing Ebenezer. "We best prepare for peace. And the end of our privileged position."

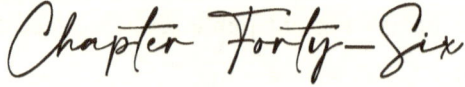

Chapter Forty-Six

Ebenezer returns from Halifax in 1817 excited about an intriguing investment opportunity—a new canal in New York spanning from the Hudson River in the East to Lake Erie. He shows Submit the map and marketing materials he received at the meeting.

"It's a wonderful thing. This could be the route we need to a market in the West."

Submit considers the route drawn on the map.

"The problem I see is that it benefits New York, Pennsylvania, but it does not benefit us. We now have an advantage in the West, because of the Saint Lawrence, as slow and difficult as it is. When they finish this Canal, New York and Pennsylvania will usurp our advantage."

She rifles through the stack of papers.

"See this pamphlet?" she says. "They tout the advantage that accrues to New England not us."

"Can we find a way to use it to our advantage? Get in on it first?"

"Perhaps but I see it taking away our advantage."

"We could invest in it."

"We would only be investing in our demise."

"What if we expand our operations into the West before it's completed? It's going to take years. What if we move operations to York? It will be an exciting time in York, as it rebuilds. William had contemplated this, why not now?"

"Why not indeed? The small obstacle of Niagara Falls."

"But if we build a place of operations in York, the Falls won't matter."

"It would be massively expensive. And we're reliant on the natural resources of Nova Scotia—the lumber, fish, minerals, plants—we lose those advantages there."

"I've never known you to overlook an opportunity or shirk in the face of a challenge."

She picks up the map.

"You are at least right about this. One day York will be the center of Canadian commerce. It's small now, but its proximity to the insatiable expansion of America will make it so. Whether we take advantage of it or not."

In 1820, Submit arranges a large party on the front lawn of Grant Hall to celebrate Joseph's tenth birthday. She invites all her extended family to celebrate.

Walking among them on a lovely afternoon embellished with intense sunshine, Submit observes with pleasure the huge family that has gathered for the event and runs through the list of kin in her mind.

The adults cluster together at tables arranged on the lawn in the shade of large oaks. The younger children play tag and blind man's bluff. Their older siblings lounge on blankets off to the side laughing at their private jokes. Submit and Lily stroll arm in arm around the property dressed in bright silk dresses from Paris, parasols on their shoulders.

"Do you think you know all of their names?" Submit asks.

Lily shrugs. "Do you?"

"I doubt it. But I'm sure you do."

"I might."

Submit looks over at a table where her brother Andrew sits with his wife Mary McPherson. "What about them?"

Lily takes a deep breath.

"Their first, Sarah, named after your mother, is eighteen. Then come Joanna, Mary, Margret, Andrew, Cassandra, James, John, and the baby Isabella."

Submit smiles.

"Now it's your turn," Lily says, pointing to Jabez's wife, Margaret McPhearson, standing alone on the lawn.

"That's easy." Submit says. "There's only four – my nephews Andrew, John, William and Oliver. It's so sad that my brother is no longer with us, unable to see his sons grow into men."

Submit and Lily take seats at a table where they can watch the children play.

"I marvel at the size of this family," Submit says. "And that we've been able to manage it all these years."

"We've been through many changes," Lily says. "You've gone from a girl, to stepmother, to mother, and now grandmother."

"It's a far larger brood than I ever imagined," Submit says. "Far larger than when I first imagined married life."

SUMBMIT

"Like a fluffle of rabbits," Lily says. "But all worth it, I hope."

"A large family has its rewards, but sometimes I 'm overwhelmed by how many of them rely on me for support.

"Your burden to carry," Lily says.

"My cross to bear."

"Your lot in life." They both laugh.

"Thank God for your help," Submit says, reaching for Lily's hand.

A gaggle of girls interrupt them. "It's time for cake," they shout in unison.

The family gathers together in the shade of a large tree for cake and lemonade and the opening of gifts. Ebenezer surprises Joseph with his gift. A three-foot, rolled-up tube of parchment tied with a ribbon.

"Open it," he says.

Joseph unties the bow and rolls out the document on the table. He appears puzzled by what he sees.

"It's a commemorative ticket," Ebenezer says. "For a journey on the Erie Canal. We'll go there together. Only part of it is done, but someday it will be a gateway to a whole new world."

Most of those gathered around greet the clever gift with applause. But Submit turns away, her smile contorted into a scowl.

Later, when they are alone in their bedroom, Submit confronts Ebenezer about his gift.

"He's only ten," she says.

"You hold him back from commerce. He's old enough to learn about the business. You won't let me take him to Europe. You won't let me give him a job at that mill."

233

Ebenezer stands and takes a gulp of whiskey, then continues. "Both are too dangerous, you say. He's too young, you say. But I say he could and should do these things so he can take over our businesses someday. If not him, who?"

"What about Abijah?"

"Abijah? He's a clever lad, but he's not up to running the business, and he's not our son."

"James."

"Won't happen. You've sent him away to Europe and now you're letting him go to New York to be a lawyer. He'll never settle down here. Besides, he's not my son."

Submit is on the verge of lashing out at this but holds back. She has learned from her skirmishes with Mary when best to let heated words cool and extinguish. She takes Ebenezer's hand and leads him to sit beside her on the bed.

"Joseph needs an education to take over. The time to bring him into the business will come."

Ebenezer squints at her and leans away.

"If we wait too long, he'll be stuck on another path, he'll have no interest. He glues his nose to the pages of so and so and such and such. When I was his age, I was off to sea, a captain's boy, learning the ways of a merchant world."

"I won't have that."

"I'm not saying he needs to do that. I'm not even taking his books away, though I'd like to."

"What are you saying?"

"Let's give him a break. He's been studying hard."

"He does chores on the farm."

"Not the same thing. Give me a month to show him this new wonder. I was younger than him when my father took me west of the Hudson, canoeing on the Mohawk, deep into the frontier of New York. I want him to experience that."

"Can't it wait? Perhaps when he turns twelve, he'll be on the cusp of manhood then. Ben Franklin was twelve when he was apprenticed and look how he turned out. We can wait until Joseph is twelve, like Franklin."

He shakes his head and rubs his forehead with his fingers.

"You will win this argument you know, no matter how long it lasts."

"I know."

"I have a condition."

"What?"

"Can we teach him more math? Bookkeeping and such? That might help both of us one day. He's good with numbers."

She kisses him, pushes him back on the bed, and lays herself on top of him.

"And you're good with me."

Chapter Forty-Seven

Three weeks before Joseph's twelfth birthday, Submit sits on the bed she's shared with Ebenezer for eighteen years. He sleeps, his breathing raspy, rattling in his hollow chest.

His eyes open. "Isn't this the year?" he asks. "Do you remember? We agreed. But I never had a chance, did I? To get him to the Erie Canal?" He collapses into silence.

Submit holds his hand and watches him sleep.

Lily enters the room. The light of the rising sun creeps around the edges of the drawn window shades. Submit gets up and joins Lily in the hallway.

Lily asks, "How is he?"

"Resting now," Submit says. "It was a restless night. I read from Psalms to calm him. He dozed off and on. Talked off and on. To me, sometimes; sometimes to imagined spirits."

"What did he say?"

"Rambling mostly, incoherent. Often as if he were talking to others and I could only hear half of the conversation. His mind was elsewhere, in the woods I think, on a river maybe. It was not clear much of the time." She looks back at him. His breathing still rattles.

"But the last thing he said was clear and definite. He said, 'Please, make him a businessman, not a bookish gnome.'"

"We know his will, have known it for years."

"Indeed."

"I'll watch for a bit. You need something to eat and some rest."

"I need to find Joseph. He should come up and say goodbye."

Lily gestures to the stairs leading down to the main floor.

"In the parlor with Huldah," she says. "Studying Latin."

Part Nine

1826

Chapter Forty-Eight

ぞ

Joseph turns sixteen and still cannot resist books. There are many in the second-floor library. He has read most of them: *Pilgrim's Promise*, *Robinson Crusoe*, *Clarissa*, *Tom Jones*, *Tristram Shandy*.

This night, on the day he is told his father's wishes for him — that he complete his formal education this year, and then devote himself to learning all aspects of the family business — he struggles with the conditions of his inheritance.

Why are these things incompatible? Why cannot they both be pursued?

He slides his fingers across the books on the library shelf. His hand stops at the spine of a book he has skimmed but never fully read, *Vindication of the Rights of Woman* by Mary Wollstonecraft. Strips of paper mark pages with underlined passages, placed there by his mother or his aunt. He opens to a tagged page and reads an underlined passage:

"If woman be not prepared by education to become the companion of man, she will stop the progress of knowledge and virtue; for truth must be common to all."

This rings true but does not go far enough. Why does that not apply equally to him? If he is deprived of a good education will that not stop the progress of his knowledge and virtue? If his mother and his aunt believe this, if they were able to take advantage of this, then how can they deny him the same opportunity?

If, as his father wanted, he is to be a success in business, should he not have an education so that he is well fit to pursue business as his father wishes? If Wollstonecraft's plan is a sound policy for a woman, then why is it not also a sound policy for a man?

Can it be that a woman cannot rise without an education, but that a man can? He cannot see how. Both should be educated, and "educated after the same model." Bring both up, do not push either down.

He studies Wollstonecraft's arguments most of the night until he falls asleep with the book open on his chest.

He wakes resolute in the morning and confronts his mother with his thoughts at breakfast.

Submit smiles. After all, the book Joseph now holds also inspired her. She looks at her son. "What is it that you want to know?"

"Everything."

She laughs.

"Try to be more specific."

"First of all, I want to know my history. Where do we come from? What made you leave America? Why did you come to Nova Scotia?"

"I was young, I had no choice, I followed my father's will."

"Then why did he leave? What forces pushed him?"

Submit sips her coffee.

"Those are good questions. Important ones. But I don't know the answers."

"So, you agree. Good. Then you must also agree I will not find those answers working at the mill."

Submit nods and rubs her eyes. She cannot deny that he is right. She also thinks, but does not say, *you will not find the answers in books either.*

Submit discusses this with Huldah when she arrives for a family visit the following week.

Huldah says, "You are hoist on your own petard, my dear. You want him to do well in business. He has demonstrated that to do so he needs an education. You in fact are an exemplar to prove his point."

"We give him a good education here."

"But now you intend to take that away from him."

"That is his father's will, not mine."

"What does he want?"

"To know his own history, as starters."

"America has finally opened up to us. We could make that trip."

"You could make that trip. I know I am not well. I don't have long to live, I fear. You are the one I trust to nurture him when I am gone. You are the one I trust to execute my will, to be our family's trustee, to be his guardian."

"I have my work, my position, my responsibilities. I'm not sure I can."

"Don't decide now. Think about it, that's all I ask."

A few days later, Submit takes Huldah aside to revisit the topic.

"When I die," she says, "I want you to take him to Boston, to Guilford. Let him discover what he wants to know about the past, and then see that he gets an education for the future. Will you do that?"

Chapter Forty-Nine

In the Fall of 1826, Huldah takes a hackney carriage from the Guysborough docks up to Grant Hall. Inside the house she encounters Lily leaving the front parlor. Lily brightens when she sees her.

"Hello darling," she says. "I'm so glad you made it." They embrace. "How was your journey."

"Fine. Long. How is my sister doing?"

"Very weak but resting. We've moved her to the parlor. Easier to accept visitors. Closer to the kitchen. I'm going to warm some broth. It's the only thing she'll eat."

"Can I go in?"

"Of course. She's awake. She'll be delighted to see you." Lily heads to the kitchen and Huldah approaches the parlor. She taps her knuckles on the door and enters.

Submit sees her and pushes herself up against the pillow.

"Is it really you?" She reaches out with her right hand and beckons her to come closer. "Sit beside me," she says.

Huldah takes a seat on the bed and leans forward, kissing her sister on the forehead.

"I am so glad to be with you. To see you again before—"

"And I you, but don't write me out of the story so soon."

"I'm sorry. I didn't mean—"

"Don't worry. It's true. Death is coming soon. I can feel it. But never mind that. You're here now, that's what matters."

Lily enters with a bowl and spoon.

"It's lovely to see you both together. You're smiling, Submit, I haven't seen you smile all week."

"I had nothing to smile about, until now."

Lily hands the soup to Huldah.

"You've revived her spirits. See if you can get her to take some of this. I'll go upstairs to make sure your room is ready."

Huldah smells the broth. Chicken. She feels the temperature of the bowl. Barely warmer than a baby's cheek.

"See my hands?" Submit says. "They tremble. Can you help me?"

"Of course."

Huldah lifts a spoonful of broth to her sister's lips.

"Not bad. Could use a bit of tarragon, though."

"I'll tell the chef." Huldah offers up another sip and Submit accepts.

"That's enough for now," she says. "Tell me about yourself. How is the University?"

"Wonderful."

"Are you happy there?"

"Very."

"What is like, to be a professor in a world of men."

"I'm a researcher, not a professor."

"What does that mean?"

"I do research for books."

"Who writes them?"

"I do, usually."

"Are they published?"

"Often."

"In your name?"

"No. Under the professor's name."

"Lily." Submit calls out as loudly as she can. "We need to start a publishing company."

There's a moment of silence.

"I don't think she hears you," Huldah says.

Submit closes her eyes as if falling asleep, then revives.

"What is it like, being a researcher?" she asks.

"Well, I have an office. A large desk. Windows overlooking the quad."

"And books?"

"Yes, lots of books."

"Have you read them all?"

"Many, not all."

"Do you have a book with you?"

"Yes, a new one, a horror story, by Mary Shelly."

"I remember. You met her years ago."

"Yes, and now she's grown and she's an author."

"Will you read it to me?"

Huldah sets down the broth, takes the book from her bag, and begins where she left off. "It was on a dreary night in November."

Before long, she sees that Submit is asleep again. She sets down her copy of *Frankenstein.*

After a time, Submit stirs, restless, and calls out, "Lily, let's do that in London. They sell books by women there."

She slips back into sleep as fast as she awoke.

Submit's outburst takes Huldah by surprise. She waits for more but Submit remains still. Huldah nods off too. The candle burns down to a stub and flickers out.

The next morning Huldah wakes at sunrise. She had returned to her own room in the night. Now she stretches and walks down the hall. Lilly keeps vigil beside the bed. Submit is asleep. Lily brings her forefinger to her pursed lips and Huldah retreats.

Submit sleeps through the day with Lily and Huldah and Joseph taking turns beside her bed. In the evening, she wakes and accepts a few spoonsful of broth, then falls back to sleep.

Later when the sky turns black, Huldah tells the others they should sleep. She will stay with her through the night and let them know if there is any change.

Later that night Submit feels a surge of life within her. Light reflecting off a full moon illuminates the room through the window. Huldah sleeps in the bed next to her. Submit does her best not to wake her as she slides out of bed and finds a firm footing on the carpet beside the bed. She goes down the hall to her study, lights a candle, sits at the desk, and begins to write.

Dearest Huldah,

I am so pleased that you returned to be here with me in my final days. Before you arrived, I finished my final will with our lawyer, and am happy to say that nothing need change now that you are here, for I hoped for and expected as much, and would have willed the same in any event. I do not have long, I know, but I am able to go in peace, a happy woman for the life I've had, and also happy for the woman you are.

We are very different aren't we, yet so much the same? I think of my life, the path I've traveled, from a state of submission, befitting the destiny of my Christian name, to a state of equality with Ebenezer, to a point of independence, blessed with much material privilege and success.

You too have found independence, I feel, although by a different route, not willing to submit but instead holding on to your convictions, as also befits your name, Huldah—hold on–as you endured the pain of dishonorable lovers, our father's rejection, and the loss of your children, alone, without family support in a distant land. It hurts me dearly that I was not there for you then, as you have been here for me since, but I am now so happy knowing that the education you have pursued has given you the independence you sought, just as you always believed it would.

When you read my will, you will see that I have named you executor, trustee of the assets and guardian of Joseph. Regarding bequests, I have been as generous as I could to all concerned. To do that fully I have instructed our lawyers to arrange the sale of our businesses and properties so that the proceeds can be paid out to all my many surviving children both by marriage and by birth.

I know Mary will not be satisfied, feeling that this was her due all along, and comes too late. There is little I can do to change her bitterness toward me over her father's death, other than to accept it with equanimity and forgiveness. Perhaps with me gone she can find peace. The money should help.

You will find that I have bequeathed to you a good bit more than five pounds and a few acres of swamp land, hopefully making up for the rude treatment you received in our father's will. Among other things, I want you to have the house for as long as you live. I ask that you provide a place in it for Lily for the rest of her life. After that it should be sold for the benefit of Joseph.

I would have liked for Joseph to carry on at the helm, but it is clear to me that his destiny is elsewhere. Like you, he is destined to seek his independence through education. See that he gets a good one. He is eager to know about our family's past. Take him to Boston where he was born and to Guilford to discover his roots and to New York to see the future. After that I would be very glad if you would find him a place at your university and guide him along.

I remember your sentiment many years ago when you returned from your difficult time in Europe and settled in with Lily and me, your sentiments inspired by Wollstonecraft, that an educated woman was the equal of an educated man, and that a properly educated man knows this. Help Joseph become that properly educated man.

Then it will be up to him to decide his future. If he wants to try his hand at business, there will be a place for him here with the new owners, but let it be his free choice. He will know then that the world is much larger than our small speck.

Tell him I love him more than he will ever know. And I love you more than I can bear. It would be nice to believe that we will all be with each other again in a better place. I hope you find me there.

I must stop now, before tears smudge my labors.

Your loving sister,

Goodbye.

She folds the pages and slides them into an envelope, writing her sister's name on the front, and leaving it leaning upright against her writing box. She leans forward pressing her hands on the table and pushes herself up from the chair. The room spins. She pauses a moment to gain her balance, then returns to her bed in the front parlor.

Huldah is startled from her sleep when her arm is grasped by a skeletal hand. Submit tugs at her, rousing her from her sleep.

"Listen," she says. "You must do this for me. I want you to write and give my eulogy. Don't let the Reverend do it. He doesn't know me like you do. No one does. You must do it. Do you promise?"

"Of course. Whatever you want."

Submit lies back in her spot on the bed, exhausted from the exertion of letter writing and effort to wake Huldah. She goes quiet again drifting away into sleep. She never returns.

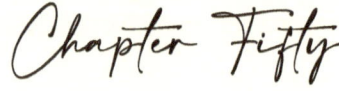

Chapter Fifty

A few days later, Huldah sits near the lectern in the front of the church. She holds a sheaf of paper in her hands, looks out at the congregation, and waits for the funeral service to begin. The church is full, crowded pews, many standing around the edges. Some gather outside watching through open windows.

The reverend signals to the choir for the opening hymn.

How happy every child of grace
Who knows her sins forgiven
This earth, she cries, is not my place
I seek my place in heaven.

When they finish, he says a prayer, then nods to Huldah. She stands and places her papers on the lectern.

"My sister Submit lived a full and rich life. She may now be in heaven, but her place was rooted in the earth, with the land and trees and rocks and animals, with the sea and fishes and ships and wind. As a young woman she took over several businesses centered in Guysborough. Expanded them. Moved forward from fisheries and sawmills, to mining, textiles and perfume, to ship building and sailing. Many of you were part of or touched by these enterprises.

But this is not what she is most remembered for. This is not why most of you are here. You are here to honor the goodness of her soul. Her kindness to others. Her devotion to her family, which extended beyond blood, to her extended family through marriage, to her employees, and to the people who knew her through the civic projects she supported.

"She achieved a full life well lived beyond any early expectations, growing through many phases: a dutiful daughter, a loving wife and mother, a successful businesswoman, to her final role as a generous benefactor to so many. Most importantly she transformed herself by choice and action, from submission, to equality, to freedom and independence. In this she became a model to so many of us who knew her.

"Submit was born in Guilford, Connecticut, near the start of the rebellion against the King, the daughter of a good man, Andrew Leete, and our sainted mother Sarah, both known and loved by many of you. Submit arrived here with her family in 1787 when she was ten years old, part of a large family, with one more still to arrive."

She pauses and points to herself with a wink. Several in the congregation chuckle.

"When she was twenty-three, she married the first great love of her life, Captain William Grant, and an existing family full of children. She embraced them all as her own and loved them dearly."

She looks up from her papers.

"Many of you are here now and can recall the warmth of her affection from that time."

Mary frowns at this, her hands balled into tight fists. She does not believe what she hears. She does not believe that Huldah believes what she is saying. The first great love of her life, indeed. The only love she saw was selfish love and adulterous lust.

Huldah continues. "After Captain Grant's death, she continued to embrace her stepchildren as her own and found the second great love of her life, Ebenezer Partridge. They became true partners in business and in life, equals in every way, even as they both shared grief over the loss of Submit's beloved husband and Ebenezer's cherished mentor. Together they expanded the business founded by Captain Grant to even greater levels of success, while they tended the large family under their care, always supported by the love and care of their trusted helpmate Lily."

Huldah ends with this: "Surely she is now in heaven, if there is one, a happy child of grace, but her place in life was on the earth with all of you whom she loved."

She folds her pages in half and leaves the pulpit to resume her seat.

Mary slides out of the pew and exits through the side door. She gulps in fresh air and stands still until she can breathe normally again. It was all too much. The canonization of Submit and Ebenezer. The failure to acknowledge their evil glee at and probable participation in the death of her father. Beloved husband. Cherished mentor. What disingenuous nonsense! The whole thing fans the embers of anger long smoldering within her into a fulgor of flames she vows to stoke until she is laid in her grave.

Chapter Fifty-One

Several months after Submit's funeral, Joseph shops at the general for provisions. Mary's daughter Ruth Ann is also in the store with her friend Agnes. They look his way, giggling. He winks at them. They rush outside.

Jospeh completes his purchase and leaves the store. He sees Ruth Ann crying nearby. Agnes is gone.

"What's wrong?" he asks.

"Nothing. I can't tell you."

"Of course you can."

She remains silent.

"Did Agnes hit you or something?"

"No, not that."

"What is it then?"

"I said I wanted to marry you."

He stifles his impulse to laugh and waits for more.

"She said I was silly, that I couldn't marry you because you're my uncle. Then she laughed at me and ran off." Ruth Ann sniffles. "Is that true?"

He places his hand on her shoulder. "Not exactly. My mother was your mother's stepmother, so I guess that makes me your uncle of sorts, although we're not related by blood. But there is another reason you can't marry me."

She pouts.

He tweaks her nose with his thumb. "Because you're only five."

"But will you someday?"

He smiles. "You will have many choices better than me. But for now, I will walk you home if you'd like?"

March 1, 1827

Dear Mr. Cavendish,

Your letter regarding your recent trip to Japan has been received with great delight. What a pleasure to hear from you after these many years. I found your list of the wishes posted by children on ema tablets at your local temple to be quite amusing, and the list of those posted by elderly adults to be quite sad. I hope your own practice has brought you the sense of forgiveness you crave. Isn't it true: when young we only want a puppy; when old, only health, happiness, and a chance to live with ease?

For my part, there has been much joy and much sadness in recent years. The sadness is the loss of my sister and her husband who have both passed away, leaving me with the joy of being the guardian of their son, my nephew, Joseph, a fine young man of sixteen. He explodes with an eagerness to learn. We will soon leave on an extended journey to the United States of America to explore our roots.

I hope you can visit our park soon and lay flowers beside my stone.

Affectionately yours,

Huldah

It is the end of the Trinity Term at King's College. Huldah has finished her duties for the summer and has returned to Guysborough to begin her travels with Joseph. They have packed enough gear for three months.

The morning of their departure is sunny and bright with sea air smelling of salt and fish. They board a schooner for Halifax, where they've booked a cabin for a four-day trip to Boston on the *Cherub*. They explore Boston for a few days, admiring Beacon Hill, the Park Street Church, and Faneuil Hall. When they reach the Customs House, Joseph consults his notes. "It is the tallest building in the United States."

Huldah takes Joseph to Harvard to observe a Latin class taught by Professor George Otis. Joseph follows along as the students translate Tully's *Discourse Upon Friendship*. She beams with pride and approval. That night they dine at the Atwood & Bacon Oyster House on Narragansetts and scallops and sarsaparilla. The next day they board a schooner for a four-day sail to New Haven.

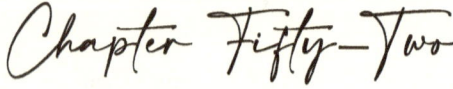

Chapter Fifty-Two

On their final day on board for the sail to New Haven, Huldah and Joseph have a simple breakfast in their cabin — hard bread, jam, slices of cheese, hot tea. Huldah reviews a small stack of letters, then turns to Joseph.

"Your uncle Jared says he will meet us at the dock this morning. Then he'll take us to Guilford to meet his family."

"Where will we stay?"

"At his house, I suppose. He says he's arranged rooms for us. That's all I know."

"They are not so far from Guysborough, only about a week by boat," Joseph says. "Why did they never visit? And why did we never visit them until now?"

"I can't say exactly. I didn't know about your uncle until after your grandfather Andrew died. Even then he was only a name on your grandfather's will. And I had no interest in America. I went to Europe instead. Then another war came, and we couldn't travel to Boston, at least not safely. After that so many years had passed."

"Did Mother know him?"

"Yes, when she was young and living in Guilford. But the family was separated by war. When our side of the family left for Canada, your uncle had his own family and stayed behind. We were separated by distance, by our loyalties, and by time."

There is a knock on their cabin door and the steward enters.

"We'll dock soon," he says.

"Our bags are ready."

"Good. I'll fetch them shortly. You're welcome to go on deck to watch the landing if you wish."

They are the only passengers on this leg of the journey and have the deck to themselves, except for the crew preparing containers to unload on the dock. Huldah and Joseph stand at the ship's railing and watch their approach to Long's Wharf. The other ships anchored in the harbor rock with the waves, their fittings clanging against the masts.

The port is busy. Men and boys load crates and luggage. Horses pull wooden wagons. Gulls fight over scraps of breakfast. Tidy buildings—two and three stories high—are set back from the water's edge and ring the harbor. Lush green hills and massive stone outcroppings stand tall in the distance.

It looks like Guysborough, but much larger.

On land, an older man dressed in a blue coat with brass buttons and tan trousers stands by an open Landau carriage. The coachman by his side holds the reins of the lead horse in a four-horse team.

The man waves and approaches alone, his unsteady gait supported by a brass-knob cane.

He removes his hat and calls out, "Sister!"

Huldah extends her gloved hand.

"Mr. Leete," she says.

"Now, now, please, Mr. Leete was our father. Call me Brother, please, or Jared."

He takes her hand, bows toward it, as if to kiss it. She feels no contact but smiles at the chivalrous gesture.

"It is such a pleasure to meet you, dear sister, such a pleasure indeed."

"I too am delighted."

"And this of course is Joseph."

He reaches out and Joseph shakes his hand. Jared turns to Huldah.

"A fine lad indeed."

"We are very proud of him," she says.

He nods to a dock porter, points to the luggage at their feet, then takes Huldah by the arm.

"We have a long ride ahead of us. Thankfully it's a lovely day. Are you hungry? You must be. I have a basket lunch waiting in the carriage."

During the ride Jared tells Huldah and Joseph about a party for them at his house on Leete Island. Most of his children and their children have come to meet their Nova Scotia kin.

"How many are there?" Huldah asks.

"Altogether I have seven children. One born every two or three years, and twenty grandchildren, at least so far. Some others are on their way, I expect. In the oven as they say."

He laughs and rubs his hands together as if he were ready to cut into a fresh apple pie.

He turns to Joseph.

"How old are you, young man.?"

"Just sixteen."

"Several of the youngest grandchildren are about your age. Lucy and Simeon are about the same if I remember correctly. Alexander, William, and Andrea close. You'll fit right in."

"Do you know all of their names?" Joseph asks.

"Don't test me, I'm sure I'll miss a few." He winks. "We could play a game after you've been with them a bit, see which of us gets the most names right. Pin the name tag on the child, or some such thing."

Jared lifts a checkered cloth from the top of the basket on the seat beside him, displaying bread, cheese, sliced meat, and apples.

"I'm getting a bit peckish," he says. "What about you?"

The carriage emerges from the woods into a flat open area with a small group of saltbox houses next to open water. Jared hands an apple to Joseph.

"This is Shell Beach. It won't be long now, only a mile or so."

The carriage soon turns on to a road lined on each side with a split timber fence. Pastureland spreads out on either side. Sheep graze in the distance.

"Here we are," Jared says. "Leete Farm, our humble home."

They ride up a hill and follow a turn in the road, revealing a cluster of buildings below in a valley, and the ocean beyond. Two large white houses flank a red barn. Off to their left a man feeds grain to a herd of cattle. The road wraps around to the right and the carriage pulls to a stop in the courtyard of one of the houses.

"You must be tired from your journey," Jared says. "I know I am. We'll show you to your room and let you get settled. The family will gather later this afternoon."

Jared helps Huldah down from the carriage and leads the way through the front door. The entry way is spare. White walls. The dark wood flooring gleams with reflected light. A portrait of an old man hangs by the front door.

"William Leete," Jared says. "Your great-great-great grandfather. Two hundred years ago. Can you imagine?"

"What did he do?"

"Many things, actually. He was the first Governor of Connecticut, for one."

Joseph turns and points to a portrait of a man with an ugly nose on the opposite wall.

"Was he also our grandfather?"

Jared chuckles.

"No, lad. That's Oliver Cromwell, a revered image from the past. He fought his King over a hundred years before our Patriots here fought ours."

Chapter Fifty-Three

Their room on the second floor is spare and clean, with two twin beds and a pair of windows with a view of trees and water. So far, everything seems so familiar to Huldah, like the house where she grew up, spacious but simple. They lie down to rest and soon fall into a peaceful sleep.

A knock on the door wakes Huldah. She answers. A boy about the same age as Joseph looks at her with pale blue eyes.

"Hello, Miss," he says. "I'm Simeon. Grandfather sent me to show my cousin around the farm. He also asked me to invite you to visit him in the front parlor."

Simeon directs Huldah to a room at the front of the house, then hustles away pulling at Joseph's sleeve.

Huldah finds Jared at a desk pushed against one wall of the parlor. He rises to greet her.

"Huldah, please come in. Care to join me for a cup of tea or something stronger?"

"What are you having?"

"Whiskey."

"I'll have the same."

He pours whiskey at the sideboard and hands her the tumbler.

"So, The black sheep finally meet."

This catches her speechless. Jared laughs.

"I only refer to our privileged position at the bottom of the heap in our father's will. Although I'd say my five shillings beats your five pounds and a chunk of swamp land by a fair margin." He takes a seat beside her and raises his glass. "What did you do to so endear you to him?"

"I ran away to visit a man in Geneva without his permission. He was furious. What about you?"

"Ah, it's a long story. The short version is that we disagreed about the War. The long story is complicated."

"That's what I came here for. To hear complicated."

"What do you know about our family's life here?"

"Not much. Assume I know nothing. I wasn't born until we got to Nova Scotia as you know, and we never talked about the past."

Jared stands and removes a stack of papers from a desk drawer. "These will help with the tale. I'll tell you as much as we can. But first you need to understand this. I sided with the Patriots. And I'm proud of it. Father had a different view, and that's the heart of our schism."

"Please tell me what you know. Start at the beginning."

He lays the papers on a low table between them. "Our father Andrew was born in Guilford, in this house in about 1731. He met my mother, and they married in 1763. He was thirty-two. She was twenty-one. I was born one year later. Things did not go well."

He lifts a document from the top of the stack of papers and hands it to her. "This is a Petition for Divorce, that he filed in 1769, when I was five years old. This part states the problem."

He points to the tight handwritten letters in the middle of the page.

"He claims that his first wife, my mother, Esther Bletchley, deserted him in 1769. Committed adultery, and lived apart from him. So he asked the court to grant him a divorce."

"And you were five at the time?"

"About that."

"What was it like?"

"My mother took me with her. I didn't know what was going on. I lived with her and a man named Thomas Arden. She was younger than my father by more than ten years. Arden was her age. I lived with them in a small house on the edge of town."

He takes back the yellowed petition and runs his index finger over their father's signature.

"I've locked my memory to most of this, but I remember that he was cruel, he'd beat me with a stick if I did something he didn't like. Usually on my back or my lower legs."

He squints and shakes his head.

"He would hit me until it drew blood. 'There, that will teach you,' he said."

"Did you tell Father?"

"I tried to. I ran away and went to him. He would listen to me but send me back to my mother and Mr. Arden."

Huldah frowns.

"He should have protected you but didn't. I can see why you might be bitter."

Jared nods in agreement.

"But I said this was complicated. There's more."

Huldah sips her whiskey and waits.

"I lived with the two of them for about four years. Hard years. No school. Ragged clothes. Alone for days with little to eat. And then she died. In 1773. I was nine. One day Mr. Arden came back to our house alone. 'She's dead,' he said, while he packed his clothes in a bag. I wanted to know how. He wouldn't say. Instead, he swapped me across the face with the back of his hand and knocked me to the floor. He fled out the door."

He pauses to contemplate his drink.

"His hand smelled like this." He holds up his glass.

Huldah waits for more.

"I was alone for days. It felt like weeks. But I know it was only a few days."

"Did you go to Father then?"

"No. I'd tried that before, and he sent me home. So instead, I waited not knowing what to do. Finally, he arrives at the house looking for me. I hid at first, but then I saw he was with a woman. It was your mother, Sarah. But I didn't know her then, but somehow her presence made me feel safe. I came out and they took me in."

"How difficult that must have been. So confusing."

"Thinking about it now, I felt like an abused dog must feel. But I didn't know that then. I didn't know anything else. Our father then was forty-one. Your mother Sarah was only nineteen, closer to my age than his. They

SUMBMIT

rescued me, that's how I saw it. She was like a big sister to me, or a saint from heaven. It was not an easy path for her to get there, though."

He refills his glass and offers her more, which she declines.

"I need some liquid courage to get through this," he says.

"And I need less, so I can remember."

"Ah, yes, most prudent." He resumes his seat. "Sarah, your mother, had married before, to a man named Minard Cockard, from New York. They married in about 1764, the same year I was born. But that too didn't last."

He hands Huldah the next set of papers from the pile.

"This is her divorce petition."

"Don't tell me he abandoned her?"

"I'm not sure. You'll see in the petition that they were together for three years. Then Cockard went to Boston to begin a sea voyage—or at least that's what he told her—and she never saw or heard from him again."

He points to the signature at the bottom of the petition.

"This was signed and granted on the 30th of August 1773. That was three months after my mother died—for causes I have never learned. And three months after I met Sarah, my new stepmother, when she and my father came to rescue me."

He pauses and Huldah waits. She sorts through the dates—a coincidence, or too close to be anything other than design? But if design, what would be the benefit? She dismisses the thought. Sometimes a coincidence is only a coincidence.

"When were they married—our father and my mother—after Esther's death?"

"Soon after in October of the same year."

She searches his face for clues. "Did you suspect something? A plan to—"

267

"No. I did at the time. But not now. I don't suspect anything now. There was nothing to gain. And her death was not required for his marriage to Sarah. I have no reason to be suspicious."

Huldah looks away through a window at the distant horizon. Is that true, that there was nothing to gain?

Jared interrupts her thoughts.

"I resented the fact that he remarried, but that did not last. My father and your mother were good to me. That is not the cause of our falling apart from each other. The falling apart did not happen until later."

Huldah focuses back on Jared. "Why then? When?"

He sets his glass on the table.

"I was thirteen when the Declaration was signed. Already caught up in the furor surrounding independence from the Crown. It seemed more important than anything. Father held me back, I was too young, we should remain neutral, it was a spat between parent and child, they would reconcile. He said all those things to keep me from running away to serve. But the parent and the child didn't reconcile. My furor in support of the Patriots grew. Father's went in the other direction." He lifts another handwritten petition from his stack. "He was called up to serve. Here's what he did."

Jared hands her the petition. She struggles to read the fainting script.

Jared points to the second page.

"This explains he would not take up arms but choose to live peaceably with all men. Notwithstanding those sentiments he was drafted into Continental Service. That was 1778. He was fifty years old, although he does not make his age an issue and given his robust health at the time, that basis would have surely failed. Instead, he asks that his frankness not be considered a crime and begs that he be exempt from service."

Jared sets the petition down on the table between them. "He was outraged when he learned that his petition had been denied. I was outraged to learn he was refusing to serve. Although I was only fourteen, we had terrible arguments about that. We each said things we came to regret. I more than him."

He lifts another document from the stack of papers. "But he did not give up. Here's his petition in 1779 to our governor Jonathan Trumbull. He asks again to be exempt and permitted to depart from the State."

He hands the petition to Huldah and wipes his brow with his kerchief.

"Again, his request was denied," Jared says. "So, he was drafted into service against his will. About this time all landowners were required to provide a list of what they owned and pay taxes. He did so, at first. But in 1781 he and others were black-listed and made liable for all damage done by the enemy on any of the town's inhabitants. Because the damage was so great, he concluded that his property would soon be taken, so he did not turn in his list for 1781 or 1782."

Huldah asks, "It was a protest, not an oversight?"

"He knew exactly what he was doing, and others did the same." Jared rises and refills his glass. "Then we learned about the Patriot victory and the Peace Treaty in 1783, but that didn't stop the problems. They took cattle and other goods from him by force. They put him in jail at his own expense. He petitioned to get his money back and to remove to the dominions of Great Britain, but this too was denied. In 1778, he petitioned the general assembly in Hartford. Here is a copy, which you will find quite interesting."

He points to various sections for her to read. Her father claimed it was his duty to take no active part by taking up arms. That he was born under allegiance to the King and never considered it justifiable to renounce that allegiance and join a constituency independent of it.

"He says he was legally exempt under the Resolution of Congress and General Washington's order. Let me read these lines, he says it better than I can—

"The present controversy is professedly for Liberty. Your Petitioner therefore cannot conceive it consistent with the Idea of Liberty, and the most Sacred Idea of it, Liberty of Conscience, to fight in a cause which although he will not be so assuming as to say is unjust yet in his conscience, he believes not to be justifiable."

Jared inspects his empty glass and sets it on the table.

"This is the heart of the problem between us. You see, I believed in the cause. So much so, that I was in the field fighting for it, and he believed that cause was not justifiable. We were unable to bridge that abyss."

There was a knock at the door. Simeon and Joseph enter. Jared turns to them.

"Hello boys."

Simeon says, "Mother sent me. She said I should ask you to join the family. Dinner is ready."

"Quite right." Jared stands with the help of his cane. "We're finishing up. We'll be down promptly."

When the boys are out of the room, he squares the pages on the table and hands them to Huldah. "Take these back to your room. Look them over. We'll find another time to talk about them."

Chapter Fifty-Four

That night, after the dinner party, Joseph goes straight to sleep when they get back to their room. Huldah sits at a desk in the corner of the room next to a lamp with the papers spread out in front of her. She makes notes to get the dates in order.

The papers raise more questions than they answer. What exactly had he done to merit prison? What had he done to be labeled a dangerous person, an open and secret enemy? Are these the sins to which he referred on his deathbed? And what of Jared, only seventeen at the time of the investigation? What did he say and do to help or harm his father during this time? What more did he know?

In the morning, Huldah finds the house deserted. The family is off to the fields, or back to their nearby houses, or still asleep. She finds Jared alone in the dining room with bread and jam and a newspaper.

He looks up when she enters.

"Ah, sister, please join me. What has hurt you more, your long fasting or your early rising?"

She smiles. That is something their father often said.

"My rising was the hardest part," she says.

Jared frowns.

"Did you not sleep well?"

"Not very, I'm afraid."

"Was the bed not comfortable? One doesn't know these things about one's guest beds, you know. Never sleep in any but my own."

"The bed was fine, but my mind was restless. I read through the papers you gave me. That on top of the family gathering."

"I didn't mean for any of this to disturb you. My apologies. But you wanted—"

"Yes, I want to know everything, but in a way, I now feel I know even less."

"How can I help?"

"How can it be that my father—our father—was a dangerous person, a secret enemy?"

"To understand that you must first understand the times. The War was approaching our doorstep. The British occupied New York and Long Island. We were near the front lines, less than a day's march, an easy target from the sea. Tempers were tense between the Patriots and the Tories.

"Before long, one wrong led to another. A band of men loyal to the Crown fought back at their mistreatment. There were night raids by that band on the farms of the Patriot supporters. Robberies, vandalism. There was a week of terror where they burned down barns every night.

"One of the barns belonged to the head of our local militia, an ardent Patriot. His daughter, Julia, only eleven, ran out to rescue her horse. Julia was burnt to cinders. The horse died too."

Huldah buries her face in her hands. "Oh. No. Was Father—"

"They were his friends. The Patriots who did it. There was never any evidence that he was with them that night. Or any night when they burned barns. But he was on their side. He was with them in spirit."

"That must have been terrible for you."

"It was for many of us."

"But you, I mean. Especially."

"We fought over it. In words only. I couldn't strike him. He was my father. But I lashed out at him with words. The worst was this: the last time we spoke I called him a coward for not confessing, and a liar for claiming that he was persecuted on, as he said, suspicion only."

"So, he was not neutral?"

"Not in my mind. And not in his heart, I'm sure."

"Do you think he was involved in other things like that? Was there blood on his hands?"

Jared paused, rubbed his own hands with a handkerchief. "I was sure of it, at the time, but I had no proof. Now? I don't know. But I will tell you what I believe. That he was capable of it."

Huldah's eyes grow wide with shock.

"I know what you're thinking," Jared says. "That the father you knew was not capable of that kind of act. But it was a different time. He was younger. Tempers were hot. He tried to stay neutral, but there were attacks on him by the Patriots, just as the Tories attacked in return. The father I knew then was capable of much, including that, and more."

She closes her eyes and raises her head to the ceiling. Then looks back at him. "Why tell me this, now?"

"I'm not sure. You wanted to know. I am older now, closer to death. I said and did things then that I regret. I suppose this is my penance for my part in the schism."

She meets this with a silence that fills the room.

"I see it comes too late," he says. "I'm sorry."

"But you don't know—"

"No, I don't."

She rises and goes to him on the other side of the table.

"Dear brother," she says. The words are almost inaudible, as she stoops to embrace him, her tear-streaked cheek against his.

Chapter Fifty-Five

T hat afternoon Jared takes Huldah and Joseph on a tour of Guilford. Simeon comes along.

The first stop is the house of William Leete, the Governor of New Haven and Connecticut. Jared tells them that William owned a town lot and the land now called Leete's Island. He arrived in the 1600s. He left England because he was a Puritan and angered at the treatment of Puritan's under King Charles. He was so opposed to the King that he sheltered the regicides. He was a man who took firm and difficult action on principle.

Jared turns to Joseph. "That man was your grandfather's great grandfather. This happened two hundred years ago."

They ride south back toward Leete Island. "This is the house of Pelatiah Leete. His grandson Simeon lived here at the time of the Revolutionary War."

Jared turns to his grandson.

"You are named after him. He was my cousin of some remove, third cousin or something like that, I'm not quite sure. He was ten years older than me, born in 1753. I looked up to him. More than my own father.

"When the War started, I was young, only fifteen. He was in the prime of his life, married, with three children. We both joined the militia to protect Guilford once again from a greedy king. One night the British invaded Leete Island from the Sound, several long boats of soldiers. Our militia turned out to fight back. The invaders burned barns and seized provisions. We tried to push them back with only our muskets. Simeon was in the lead pushing them back to their boats. They retreated to the sea, firing back at us as they got in their boats. Simeon was hit. I was nearby. I watched him fall. We ran to him. I helped others carry him back to the house. We laid him on a downstairs bed. We were all soaked in his blood."

Jared bites his lower lip, then continues. "He died the next day."

Huldah reaches out to hold Jared's hand. "How terrible for you. I can't imagine."

"Follow me," he says. He leads the visitors to a spot in the field behind Pelatiah's house marked with a single large stone.

"This is where we buried him."

Jared turns to Huldah. "If you want to know why I hate the British, this is why."

Back in the carriage, they head toward a rocky promontory jutting into the waves. They ventured to the edge, a beach below them, salt marsh behind them, and the edge of a forest in the distance.

"This is Sachem Point," Jared says, "the site where we initiated our last attack of the War. Our regiment was supplemented by militia from other parts of the colony, about three hundred men in all. We had about thirty whaleboats staged on the beach. There was no moon that night, so it was as dark as coal after the sun went down. We lit torches to guide us off the beach, then rowed by instinct across the Sound to the enemy camp. We could see campfires as we approached. We found the British soldiers drunk and silly. Many sleeping on the ground. All separated from their weapons stacked by their tents. We had an easy time of it, rounding up the soldiers as prisoners and looting their stores. That night we were certain we would win the War, that we could not be beaten by soldiers such as those."

Joseph walks closer to the head of the bluff and looks out across the water. Jared says, "The land is too far away to see unless the sun is right and air is clear, but not on a misty day like this."

"Is that New York?"

"Long Island, part of New York." Jared points to the right. "The City is over there. A massive, busy place, with thousands and thousands of people living on an island. By choice at that."

"We're headed there next," Huldah says.

"What shall we see?" Joseph asks.

"The future," Jared says. "Tall buildings. Harbors thick with ships from all parts of the globe. People speaking languages you've never heard. Free black men dressed better than a politician on Sunday. Fine ladies looking like they've just returned from Paris, dressed in the latest fashions. Businessmen rushing to the stock market. The place vibrates with life."

Chapter Fifty-Six

Huldah and Joseph walk north from Battery Park up Broadway following directions in a letter from Joseph's half-brother James Grant.

Joseph points to his left then reads from the letter. "At Trinity Church you may find it interesting to notice the burial plot for Alexander Hamilton."

They visit the grave, then continue up the street. Men and women rush by. Broadway is bustling with carriages and wagons. The red brick buildings stand close together. For Joseph, the rest of the world—Guysborough, Halifax, Boston, Guilford—seem quaint, peaceful, and puny in the face of the vigor he sees and feels here.

Soon the residential brownstones give way to a large open common and the long marble facade of the New York Town Hall. Joseph reads again from the letter: "At the park you will see City Hall on your right. They say President Jefferson hated this building, found it gaudy and ugly. I too favored Latrobe's more refined classical design, but this seems to suit the City. Continue north and turn right at Reade Street."

Farther along, the park surrounding City Hall is replaced by rows of townhouses. Joseph reads: "You will see on your right, a well-kept residence with a tidy front garden and a well-polished brass knocker on the front door—a lion's head. We're the house next door, the one in need of painting and a new railing on the upstairs balcony, a modest two-and-a-half story residence with cracked stone lintels and two rather severe dormers poking through a peaked slate roof, housing the law offices of William D. Craft on the first floor, and my private room in the attic."

James, a young man of twenty-four with muttonchops and peaked lapels, answers Joseph's knock on the door.

"Bother," he shouts, crushing him in a bear hug.

He greets Huldah more gingerly as she steps forward to plant a kiss on his cheek. He invites them to sit in the front room facing the street. Joseph notices signs of better times—a stain on the rug, a frayed cushion, a broken Dutch tile on the mantle.

James pours cups of tea from a pot on a table between the front windows. Mr. Craft is away on business so he's free for the day and can offer them lunch and his full attention.

James asks about their travels and the family behind in Canada. Huldah shares news of his siblings, all are well and doing fine. Joseph reports on the visit to Guilford, then asks James about his life in New York and work for Mr. Craft.

"It's all quite fascinating," James says. "I'm learning about politics and law. The machinations of both are like waging war without guns."

"Do you plan to follow your father into the military?"

"I doubt it. I've trained to be a lawyer, not a soldier, but I've grown very keen on politics, so who knows what the future holds." He pours more tea into their cups. "Another thing I'm keen on is the history on display in New York. So much has happened here. I've planned to show you some of it, starting with lunch, if you're up for it."

James takes them by cab to Fraunces Tavern and leads them to a corner table on the second floor.

The tavern owner, aided by a young waitress, serves their meal, beginning with mugs of ale and bowls of turtle soup.

James waves his hand around to call attention to the surroundings.

"There is much history here," he says. "The British surrendered in Virginia, thanks to help the Patriots received from the French, but the War ended here. When the British evacuated New York, Washington gathered in this very room with his officers for a final toast of victory."

Joseph asks, "Wasn't your father in New York?"

"Indeed, he was," James says. "I was only a baby when he died, of course, so I heard no stories from him. But since then, I've learned about his time as a soldier from others. He was stationed on Staten Island when the War ended. Relocated to Manhattan to help with the evacuation. And left as part of the exodus to Nova Scotia. In fact, I've learned that this very tavern played an important role in the settlement of our town."

"How so?" Huldah asks.

"The hearings to determine which slaves had earned freedom took place here," James says. "Those with a valid claim sailed away to freedom, many to Nova Scotia. In a way, Guysborough began in this room, when the Guy Carleton granted freedom to thousands of negroes and sent them to Nova Scotia. A soldier named Samuel Birch ran the hearings."

Joseph responds to this fact. "So, that's where Bircher town in Nova Scotia gets its name?"

"Exactly, named after him. Birch prepared a directory of the Negro loyalists. The original is in London. We would find some of our neighbors on the list, I reckon, no doubt the names of Miss Lily's family."

The waitress removes the dessert plates.

James says, "Would anyone care for coffee?"

Joseph is quite impressed. The fancy lunches, an important job, new knowledge of the past and the future of politics. He finds it most enticing.

As their lunch ends, James says he has something else he wants to show them, if they have time.

Huldah sees the interest in Joseph's eyes and is glad to see him absorb James's commentary on the past. They head north by carriage.

When they pass Wall Street, James says, "Imagine this, Joseph, when the Dutch came here two hundred years ago, this was the end of the town of New Amsterdam. There was a wall of timbers here, a crude barricade to protect the colony from attack. This area north of the wall became farmland."

James sends the driver to the top of Varick Avenue.

"We are now on land that played an important role in American history."

At the corner of Varick and Charlton they stop in front of one of the largest mansions Joseph has ever seen.

"This is Richmond Hill. Washington used this as his headquarters at the start of the War, until the British drove him off island. After the War, the capital of the United States was in New York and John Adams lived here when he was vice president. After that, Aaron Burr bought the mansion and lived here when he was vice president. I've heard a lot about him from Mr. Craft. They were law partners. Shall we walk around?"

"He must have had a very large family," Joseph said. "To live in such a large house."

"Actually, it was only him, his wife and his daughter Theodosia. But they had large parties and hosted many visitors."

"Does he still live here?"

"No. All that happened before we were born. After he shot Hamilton, his fortunes collapsed. He sold this to creditors and eventually Jacob Astor bought it."

Huldah waits in the carriage as James takes Joseph for a walk around the grounds. Joseph is glad for the time alone with James.

"I have never talked to you about your father's death," Joseph says. "Would you mind talking about it now?"

"I was only one when it happened. I don't know any more than you do."

"But I'd like to know what you think. You must know that Mary still blames my father and mother, even though they are both dead."

"I know she feels that way, but I've never accepted what she says. Look, I didn't know my own father. Your father is the only father I've known."

"Do you think he killed him?"

"I don't know if he did or not. But you ask what I think. I think that he did not and could not have done so."

"Why not?"

"Many reasons. First, from what I saw and heard, he admired Captain Grant, considered him a friend, loved him even. Most of what I know about my father was told to me by Ebenezer. I saw no ill will in him, just the opposite in fact. Second. Well, let me show you why. Something Mr.

Craft taught me. Stand here close to me. Look me in the eye. Are you ready? Now turn and walk ten steps away from me."

As Joseph walks, James also walks ten paces in the opposite direction. "Now turn. Stand sideways, right side facing me. Stretch out your arm. Imagine you are holding a loaded pistol. Imagine you hate me. Do you feel it?"

Joseph stands as directed.

"In a moment, one of our seconds says, 'fire at will.' Can you pull the trigger?"

Joseph's hand is shaking. "Yes, I think so."

"Fine, now close your eyes. Imagine I am your friend. That you love me. Fire at will."

Joseph closes his eyes. His arms start to shake. "I can't," he says, dropping his arm to his side. "I can't do it."

"Fine, now come close to me." They both walk back to the starting point. "Come closer, so close that you can touch me. Look me in the eye. Good. Now close your eyes. Imagine you know me, that you're holding something heavy, a hammer perhaps. Imagine that you want to kill me." James steps back. "Now, do it, try to swing at me and kill me with the hammer."

Joseph stands for a moment with his arm raised.

"Go ahead, swing at me as hard as you can."

Joseph drops his arm.

"They say it's easy for a man to kill a stranger in War. It's your duty. It's harder to kill a man you know in a duel. Even when you're twenty yards apart. Even when the Code Duello requires your best effort to do so. It's hard to kill someone you know close-up. Someone who is not attacking you in the heat of passion or hatred. Especially if you are not a killer, if you have never killed before.

"I believe Ebenezer—I call him our father, because that's how I think of him—I believe he was an innocent. He was never a soldier. He had never killed before. And so, I don't think he could have killed him."

He rests his hand on Joseph's shoulder.

"Did you see how your arm trembled, how you hesitated?"

Joseph nods, then looks straight at James. "Have you fought a duel?"

James nods, confirming he has.

"Why?"

"I was stupid. Outraged at an insult. I can't remember."

"Did your hand shake?"

Huldah walks toward them and shouts out, Joseph! "What are you two doing?"

Before she reaches them, James stretches his arm forward with his finger pointing at Joseph's heart.

"No, it did not," he says. His hand stays steady, and his eyes go cold. "I pulled the trigger before I heard the explosion of the other man's pistol. I realized that I had not been hit. I stayed steady, watching him fall to the ground. I knew then that I had honored the Code, won the duel, and was not concerned if he was dead or not. Either way I was at peace."

"Was he dead?"

James shakes his head. "Only wounded."

Chapter Fifty-Seven

That night Joseph and Huldah sit in the second-floor parlor at their New York lodgings. Huldah sips from a small glass of Madeira while Joseph prods the fire with a poker. Huldah hears the fire crackle, feels its warmth on her cheeks and sees the streetlamps flicker through the windows facing the street.

Joseph had been out for the evening with James and a few of his law clerk friends. He smells of spilled beer and is moody. She asks about his evening. He says they had dinner at a place called the Bridge Cafe.

"Was there ale?"

"Of course."

"And girls?"

"Yes."

"It doesn't sound like a place for proper ladies?"

"It wasn't," he says.

Huldah leaves it that. She doesn't want to know more. Her nephew is a man now, able to decide on such things for himself. She changes the subject.

"That demonstration of yours today at Richmond Hill, it seems to have made quite an impression. A good one, I hope."

"I wanted to know what he thought. He tried to make me understand how hard it is to be a killer. But I'm not sure."

"I sense that."

"You heard him when you came up to us, didn't you?"

"He was telling you he shot a man in a duel."

"Yes. But more than that. It was his steady hands and steely eyes. That haunts me. He meant me to see he could be a killer. If he could be, then maybe father could too. Maybe I could."

"I don't believe that. He's bragging. Showing off. You know he's like that. Has been so since he was a little boy. You can't believe him. Besides, James carries the blood of Captain Grant in his veins, the blood of a soldier. Your soul springs from a different source. You are brothers, but only by half, you are not the same."

"But Aunt Mary believes he did. She won't let it go. She's like a hungry dog with a bone. She won't let go."

"There was an inquest, you know. No charges issued. That should be enough. It is for most people. But I know it's not enough for your Aunt Mary. I've known her all my life, we were friends as children, but that ended when my sister married Captain Grant. I didn't understand at the time. But now I can see that Mary was jealous and resentful even then. She thought Submit was taking her father from her. That grew into the belief that my sister and Ebenezer conspired to kill Grant. She's clung to that belief for over two decades."

"I can see that. But I'm still troubled by it. Like any son, I want my father to be a hero, to be perfect, to be my idol. It is painful to see that someone in our family thinks he's a monster. Everyone else could tell him that it wasn't so—you, Mother, Lily, even James—but it still gnaws at me, that she thinks the same of me."

"I know what it's like for others to think you are a monster. It's a hard twist of fate. There are things in my past that I don't talk about, that caused others to think ill about me. One day I may tell you more, but not now. All I can say is I understand that burden."

"How does one deal with it?"

"I can answer only for myself, from my own experience. I have suffered from that public view, to be sure. Seen my reputation tarnished. For a time, I thought my work might overcome that, but it did not come to pass. In the end, I could only do what we all can do. Learn that the adverse opinion of those who do not know me can cause no harm, and I can rest in the comforting arms of my family and true friends. Can you do that too?"

He shrugs, turns away, and pokes at the fire. Finally, he says, "What's next?"

"Back to Nova Scotia. So you can attend King's College in the autumn."

"So, you can keep an eye on me?"

"Yes, so I can keep both eyes on you."

MARK PARTRIDGE

Part Ten

1838

Chapter Fifty-Eight

In the early Spring of 1838, Huldah works on a history of the Mi'kmaq language in the study at Grant Hall during her break before the Trinity Term begins at the University. The shelves around sag with books. Her back faces the view through the window of the ice floes on the estuary. She writes notes in the margins of a thick government report about the indigenous people of Canada. A stack of earlier works by Father Christian LeClerc and Pierre Maillard rest on the desk to her left.

Joseph raps his knuckle on the door frame. Huldah sets aside her notes and peers at him over her reading glasses. He takes a seat in front of the desk.

"I got a letter from James. He says he reckons he'll move from New York to Washington. Take a spot at the White House as a secretary to the new Secretary of Treasury."

"Sounds like a wonderful opportunity. His father would have been proud if he were still alive."

"I don't know. I would think his father wanted him to be British soldier, like he was, like his older brother John was. Not a clerk with a job at a desk."

"That sounds like you talking, not him."

"Why? Do I sound restless?"

"Yes, sound and act. You've been back from university for almost six years. The accounting work at the company doesn't suit you. Or interest you. Is that it?"

"That's not it. Father wanted this for me. I've made peace with my lot."

"Then what? A girl? Are you in love? Finally?"

The Queen's envoy takes fifteen days to carry news of Queen Victoria's coronation from London to Guysborough, triggering a local celebration at the waterfront.

Absent from the town's festivities, Joseph and Ruth Ann Scott celebrate on their own, lying naked on the rumpled sheets of a wooden bed in a rustic cottage room. Her blond hair drapes across his chest as she listens to the beating of his heart. She is on the cusp of womanhood, still glowing with youth. He bears the rough whiskers of a man a decade older. His arm wraps around her, his hand stroking the hair on the back of her head. In a swift motion, she rolls over on top of him and turns to face him, her lips inches from his.

"Now you have to marry me." She smiles and stares into his eyes.

"Gladly Miss Scott," he says. "I thought you'd never ask, but—"

"But what?" she shouts.

"I am afraid your mother will refuse."

"She's not the one getting married."

"Nevertheless—"

"I know. We can't marry and live our lives in this small town unless she approves."

"Exactly," he says. "And I fear she won't."

"She will. She must. I'll talk to her first, before you ask for permission."

"She's never liked me, you know."

"It's not you, Joseph. It's your parents. And it's a thing of the past, whatever it was, and you've been on your own for years."

"But 'the sins of the father are to be laid upon the children.'"

"That's sounds like something you read in school."

"The Merchant of Venice. Shakespeare."

"I like the Ezekiel better," she says. "Reverend Jones said it in his sermon just last Sunday. 'The son shall not bear the iniquity of the father.'"

"I hope you're right."

"Of course I'm right. Mother cannot hold the past against you, you will see." He rolls her over so he's on top of her.

"And what can I hold against you?" he asks.

"Your body will do nicely." She pulls his head closer until their lips touch in a long kiss.

Ruth Ann goes to see her mother. She tells her she has fallen in love, that she wants to get married.

"That's wonderful, darling," Mary says. "It's time you married. I didn't get married until I was twenty-two, an old maid some thought. But I wasted no time, as you were born nine months later almost to the day. So, you are at a good age, if you have a suitable suitor. But don't tell me who. Let me guess. Is it young squire Hastings? I saw the two of you at the dance last month, you looked quite pleased with his company. It would not surprise me if he has asked for your hand."

"No Mother, it's not him at all."

"Master Maguire, then. He came by last week asking to see you."

"No, neither of those boys."

"Who then?"

"You know him well, Mother. He's a fine man and we are in love. Can't you guess?"

Mary is afraid that she knows the answer. But she's unwilling to say the name out loud, so she says nothing and hopes her fear is not true.

"It's Joseph, Mother. He is not like the boys in town. He's a successful man, as you know, he can support us on his own and I love him."

Mary still says nothing. This is her biggest fear, that her daughter would want to marry the daughter of her father's murderer. He would be a perfect match if not for the sins of his parents. But the prospect of her daughter marrying their son reinflames her old animosity.

"He will come to see you soon. Please say you approve, Mother. Please."

Mary gets up from her chair and steps away.

"Tell him not to come," she says.

"What?

"I will not approve."

"I can't believe what I am hearing, Mother. Why would you say that?"

"There are many reasons."

Ruth Ann stands, her arms folded tight across her chest.

Mary continues. "He is too old. You should find someone closer to your own age."

"I don't want a boy."

294

"You're his niece, for god sakes. The church will not approve."

"We're not related by blood. I've already checked on that with Reverend Jones."

"And I will not approve because he is the son of the man who killed my father."

"How can that matter? Didn't grandfather die more than thirty years ago, before Joseph was even born? I know you think that, but you have no proof. Others say it's not true and say you're crazy. Besides, the Bible says, 'the son shall not bear—'"

"I know what the Bible says. It also says, 'I am a vengeful god visiting the iniquities of the father on the children, and on their third and fourth generations.'" You see, I am not crazy. I too am vengeful, and I will blame the sins of that man on his son."

"But Mother, please, he is innocent."

"Say no more, I will not approve."

"It's not fair."

"No more, I said. I forbid you to marry him. That's final."

Ruth Ann breaks into tears, and rushes from the house.

Chapter Fifty-Nine

Lily walks down the path from Grant Hall to town carrying a basketful of fresh bread. She passes by a grove of large oaks near the edge of town. Ruth Ann sits on a log bench alone in the middle of the trees. Lily walks closer and hears her sobs.

"Ruth Ann," she says in a gentle voice. "What's wrong dear?"

"My mother."

"She loves you. What causes this?"

"I'm in love."

"Why, that's wonderful."

"With Joseph."

"I thought so."

"And I want to marry him."

"Don't tell me. Your mother says you can't."

Ruth Ann sniffles and nods her head.

"She says he's too old and I'm his niece and his father—" She clasps her hands to her face. "She says his father killed her father."

Lily holds her tighter and rocks her as she would a young child in distress.

Ruth Ann relaxes into her embrace and dries her eyes on the sleeve of her dress. "What shall I do?"

"I'm afraid there's not much you can do, darling. But perhaps I can."

"What can you do?"

"I'm not sure. But I've known her all her life. I might be able to think of a way to help."

Ruth Ann's face brightens with hope. "Would you?"

"Of course, I'll try. You and Joseph may be a good match. I love you both with all my heart." She wipes a tear from Ruth Ann's cheek with her thumb. "I changed his diapers as I changed yours. Nothing would make me happier than to see you two married."

Lily sits alone in her room in Grant Hall. What can she say to get Mary to change her mind? She removes George's coarse iron cross from the wooden box she keeps in the back of a bureau drawer.

Now more than three decades later he may be the solution to the discord Mary feels about Ruth Ann's desire to marry Joseph. That marriage is all that matters now. It could bring together two sides of a family that she has been with and loved for most of her life.

She will tell Mary that she knows the truth. That Ebenezer did not kill William.

She could tell Mary that William's death was only an accident. But Mary would not believe that. She held him in her arms, covered in his blood. She will not accept that her father could have died in such a gruesome way by accident.

"Who did it" Mary will demand to know. "Who had cause?" Lily could say that she did because William had tried to rape her. She could take the blame. Mary might believe that Lily had a motive. After all, she witnessed William's drunken advances. But could she believe that Lily was capable of murder? Lily could not believe it herself. She could not picture herself with the courage to murder anyone. And she could not picture herself with the strength to overcome Captain Grant. Even at fifty he was stronger and more fit than most men. Mary would not believe her if she took the blame.

But she might believe that Lily's husband did it. Lily could tell her that George had motive because he believed Captain Grant had tried to rape Lily and had become enraged. He was motivated by jealousy and revenge. She could place the blame on him. What does it matter now?

It will be hard for Mary to face this, to accept that her father was killed because he tried to rape Lily. But it could be the truth—the scenario fits all the facts—her husband could have done this.

Whatever the truth may be, she can say she knows this because he confessed the murder to her, told her about his confrontation with Captain Grant in the sawmill, that they argued, that he went into a rage, that they struggled and he hit him with a board causing him to fall against the whirling saw blade, causing his blood to spill and pool on the bare floorboards of the mill.

She puts the letter and the cross back in her box and thinks about the deaths of those she has loved, her husband, William, Ebenezer, Submit, and the graves of all their dead children. She will do this because love is more important than truth.

Chapter Sixty

Mary greets Lily with a hug. She becomes a girl again in the presence of Lily, recalling the days she would tag along as Lily did her family's chores. She would try to help, but of course she was more nuisance than help, tolerated by Lily out of duty—it was her job—out of kindness—it was her nature—and out of the love that still binds them together. She has been like a mother to her all her life. More than Submit, and more than her own mother, who she knew for only ten years before she died.

They chat a moment about their health and the news of the town, until Lily changes the subject.

"Let me get to the point of my visit today. I spoke with Ruth Ann yesterday."

Mary leans back in her chair.

"She told me she wants to marry Joseph." Lily reaches her hand out to touch Mary's. "She was in tears because you refused to permit it. Is that so?"

Mary pulls back her hand. "You know the reason."

"I know your thoughts on Submit and Ebenezer."

"So, you know why I could never consent."

"That's why I'm here. There are things you need to know. Things I've kept hidden. But it's time for me to make you know the truth."

"What can you know that I don't know?"

"I know that despite all you think Ebenezer did not kill your father. Ebenezer and Submit had nothing to do with his death."

"And I suppose you know who did. Don't tell me it was an accident."

"Remember for yourself what things were like then. Submit was with child. Your father was lonely and frustrated. You saw this. You tried to protect me. Even though you were only a child. But you weren't always there. There was a night, your father finished a bottle after dinner and came into the kitchen while I was cleaning up. He made advances, I refused, and he hurt me."

Mary listens in silence. She can imagine these events, see them in her mind.

Lily takes a seat beside Mary. "I told my husband afterwards. I had to. I had a bad bruise. I didn't blame your father. I understood. I knew what he was going through. But my husband didn't understand, he was furious, out of control. He confronted your father in the mill, they fought, and—"

"How could you know this?"

"He came to me afterwards. He said he hadn't planned to kill him. He wanted to tell him to leave me alone. This is why he left for Sierra Leone." Lily reaches out to Mary with both of her hands.

Mary rejects her outreach, stands, wrings her hands. Can this be true? She paces back and forth, then turns to Lily and smiles.

"Nice try," she says, "but I know what you're doing."

"I'm only telling you what happened."

"Why tell me this now? Why not years ago?"

"I don't know. I should have. But I thought you wouldn't believe it. Or that you would hate me if you knew, because I told my husband what had happened. Because I was the cause."

"But why now?"

"Because you are letting your quest for revenge ruin your daughter's life."

Anger rises in her chest and she lashes out. "What business is that of yours?"

"You know the answer to that. How can you even ask such a question?"

Mary waves her hands in front of her as if fighting off spirits.

"No!" she shouts. "That's enough. I won't listen to it. I won't accept your story or tolerate your interference."

"You can hate me because of this if you choose, but you should not hate Ebenezer or Submit. They both loved William in their own ways, and they both loved you as well. You cannot let your feelings, your mistaken feelings, get in the way of the happiness of Ruth Ann and Joseph. Let yourself open your heart and you will know this to be true."

Mary takes a breath and regrets her harsh words. She remembers when her father dallied with Lily. She can even accept that was not the only time. She could see her father's frustration, arising from Submit's focused attention on her children and from Ebenezer's attractive magnetism.

Mary starts to sob.

"I don't know what to think. They still—"

Lily comes around the table and embraces her.

"Even if you still believe that Submit and Ebenezer betrayed William, does it still matter? Does that betrayal, if it happened, extend to Joseph? Is it cause to stand in the way of Ruth Ann's happiness?"

Mary presses her tear-streaked cheek against Lily's shoulder while Lily pats the back of Mary's head.

"Think about this," Lily says. "What would your father want for his granddaughter?"

That night, Mary goes to the graveyard at sunset. She pauses at the gate where the white picket fence surrounds the graves, the final resting place for most of her extended family. She follows a narrow path toward the center of the collection of graves. Her father lies beneath a simple marker that bears his name, age, and the bookend years of his life. She lays a bouquet of yellow daffodils at the foot of the gravestone and then kneels beside the grave.

Her father would want his granddaughter to be happy. He was a noble man. He would say a soldier who wins in battle forgives his foe, returns his horse and rifle, and sends him home. He would say forgive those who sin against you. And he would forgive his murderer.

Or he might say there is no sin to forgive, that he was not murdered, that sometimes an accident is only that. He might say instead that the best tribute for his death would be to have his granddaughter marry the son of the woman who inherited his estate and bore him children, thereby uniting his family of descendants.

Is that enough? Is that sufficient for her to grant her blessing?

Her thoughts at a loss, she asks, *Father, what should I do,* and waits for an answer. Her father taught her this when she was a child. When you don't know what to do, just ask the question, and wait. The answer will come to you. She had forgotten this over the years. Ever since her mother died, she had become too certain of her own convictions to ask for guidance, but she tries now.

She waits for the answer, but none arrives. She does not hear her father's voice. His spirit does not speak to her. But then in a flash, she knows. She hears no voice and thinks no thoughts, but her heart knows.

Part Eleven

1840: The Final Letter

Chapter Sixty-One

September 24, 1840

Dearest Submit,

Why am I writing to you now? Why am I writing a letter that you will never read? That no one will ever read? That I will burn as soon as it is finished? You see, there are things I've never told you—even in my thoughts—that still gnaw at my soul. Perhaps if I write this down and burn it, I need never think about our father's final wishes again. Or my prayers for freedom from these troubling thoughts will be granted. As when a Shinto priest burns ema tablets that have been hanging at a temple for years.

So much has happened since we tucked you in the ground fourteen years ago. I have come to your graveside as often as I was able. Left flowers, burned incense, talked to you. Do you know that I've been there? Do the dead know such things? If so then you know that Joseph has grown up to be a fine man and has married Ruth Ann Scott.

The surprise is Mary. She stood in the way at first, as you would expect, but then changed her ways, I know not why, and gave up her vendetta against you and Ebenezer, at long last, and found it in her heart to bless their marriage. By all appearances she gave up her anger in time to enjoy two years of peace before we too laid her in her grave. Sadly, she did not live long enough to meet her grandson and yours, who they named Albert Marshall Partridge. It is quite ironic that her blood and is now united with yours in the body of that darling boy.

Mary suffered so much from her father's untimely death, and from blaming you for it, and from the transfer of her father's estate to you and instead of to his rightful heirs, as she saw it. Part of me understands this, having been honored so meagerly in our father's will. You know all this, of course, but I think you would be surprised that your generous bequests of your estate, which you had grown so cleverly after William's death, also caused her pain, pain that arose from the fact that your generosity made it so hard for her to hate you. All the family was grateful, so much so that she could not feel otherwise, and that was so painful to her. She harbored that resentment along with her other resentments for these many years. Which is why it is so surprising – and so welcome – that she abandoned them and consented to the marriage of her daughter to your son.

I believe she died in peace.

And this finally takes me to the thing I can't forget, now that all who were on hand at the time have passed on – Father, Ebenezer, you, Abijah, Mary, George. Lily lives on but she does not know. So only I am left to forget, the forgetting of which is the thing I would wish to write on my Shinto tablet.

I am glad that no one knows our father's secret, except me, which he confessed to me on his death bed as the final statement of his will, which I have honored with my silence so that no one else knows the terrible bloody fact that he...

Her pen runs dry, and she can write no more. A force takes over her hand, paralyzes it. Her mind becomes blank like the sky, and she sees clouds of thought float by, a veil over the midnight moon, bearing these words: *no one can ever know.* And her acceptance of those words at last sets her free.

- THE END -

Author's Note

*S*ubmit is a work of creative fiction inspired by true events and real people.

I discovered these ancestors through the faintest of clues. My Great Aunt Jessie Partridge compiled a Partridge Family history when I was a child, tracing our ancestry to Joseph Arlington Partridge, a merchant and shipper who worked for some time in Nova Scotia and moved to Wisconsin via the Erie Canal.

But the family tree stopped there until years later, when I obtained a long letter penned by Joseph's eldest son, Albert Marshall, with the cryptic line stating that his father's "mother was married twice first to a man named Grant."

The final key to identify these ancestors appeared in *Guysborough Sketches and Essays* by A.C. Jost (1950), which documented the marriages of Submit Leete, first to Captain William Grant, and second to Ebenezer Partridge. This led to original documentation—wills, property transfers, marriage records, grave sites and court petitions—confirming the bare facts of their life in Nova Scotia, New York and Connecticut, and well as my direct descent from Joseph Arlington Partridge and his parents Submit and Ebenezer; and from Ruth Ann Scott, her parents Mary Grant and Abijah

Scott, and her grandfather Captain William Grant. Nevertheless, the historical record of these lives is scant, leaving the rest to imagination.

About the Author

Mark Partridge is a former lawyer turned writer. His latest work, Submit, marks the beginning of a series of historical novels inspired by the rich tapestry of his colonial ancestry—featuring pilgrims, puritans, soldiers, ministers, missionaries, and a Salem witch. With over three decades dedicated to the study of his family history, Mark brings a unique depth and authenticity to his storytelling.

He is a graduate of Harvard Law School whose legal career spans across private practice, academia, and arbitration. As an internationally recognized legal expert, he has penned three books and numerous articles on various legal issues, establishing himself as a thought leader in the field. He resides in picturesque southwest Michigan with his wife, where he continues to explore the intersection of history and law through his writing.

www.ingramcontent.com/pod-product-compliance
Lightning Source LLC
Chambersburg PA
CBHW051958240626
47153CB00005B/1803